1 - 25 - 22

GREETINGS KATE —

THIS ONE IS FOR YOU!

David Gross

THE NEW YEAR'S RESOLUTION

Boogie.WOogie.PRODS @ gail.com

THE NEW YEAR'S RESOLUTION

When a Snotty Marketing Executive and
a Hillbilly Are Forced Together During a
Snowstorm . . . Anything Can Happen!

DAVID CREPS

The New Year's Resolution

When a Snotty Marketing Executive and a Hillbilly Are Forced Together During a Snowstorm . . . Anything Can Happen!

Published by Boogie Woogie Books and David Creps
ISBN: 978-1-7354725-6-0

FREE BONUS BOOK!

Get a FREE copy of David Creps' hilarious television pilot:

ONE MORE FOR THE ROAD

This is the story of the Cranberrys–a small group of eccentric individuals living on a breathtakingly beautiful mountainside near Lake Tahoe.

The center of activity is Randy Cranberry. Relentlessly optimistic, he truly believes that he has written a movie script that holds the solution for "preventing the human species from continuing down its current, rapid, and obvious path to total and everlasting destruction." He spends a part of every day strategizing on how to get this script into Steven Spielberg's hands.

Libby Cranberry is Randy's wife, a sixty-five-year-old Chinese woman who claims she is less than sixty-two-and-a-half years of age. She is also notably superstitious and–to her husband's constant dismay–is more than willing to give him a plentiful amount of unsolicited advice, at any hour, day or night.

And then there is Penrod Cranberry, who is three years younger than his brother Randy. One might describe him as a dapper old hippie who lives alone in a two-story, aspen-tree cabin, constructed on the large flatbed of a 1946 Dodge truck straddling a beautiful mountain stream.

Penrod's primary interest in life is the same as Randy's: to make the most insulting remark possible . . . as often as possible . . . to each other.

Get your FREE copy of *One More for the Road* here:

www.BoogieWoogieBooks.com/bonus

This book is dedicated to whomever can get it read by Anna Kendrick or Milana Vayntrub.

CHAPTER ONE

Once upon a time, in 1989, a couple of days before the new year, in a trendy Seattle shopping district, people were idling away an afternoon drinking coffee in outdoor cafes and watching sailboats skim through a calm bay surrounded by beautiful homes with large 'view windows' and vast white decks with telescopes on them.

In a vibrant fish market, sturdy men wearing leather aprons launch enormous, freshly-caught fish from one bin to another, entertaining the tourists.

In a nearby canyon, two 'expensively casual' dressers, Harold Benson and Al Babbit, glide through a series of turns in a shiny black Mercedes convertible. Harold, the driver, lifts his chin to get the best angle on the sun's rays. Al is stretched out across the back seat, perusing *Variety*. *Vanity Fair*, *The Hollywood Reporter*, and *People* magazines are scattered within his reach.

Janice and Heather, a pair of pretty women in their mid-thirties, jog along a path parallel to the ocean. Heather wears scruffy red sweat pants and a loose gray sweatshirt. Janice wears an expensive turquoise jogging outfit with matching shoes and headband.

The Mercedes leaves the canyon and pulls into an ocean-side parking lot.

Harold looks at his wristwatch and turns off the engine.

Janice also looks at her wristwatch before she and Heather turn off the jogging path and head for the Mercedes. They arrive panting, and Janice gives Harold a wobbly kiss as she runs in place.

Without leaving the driver's seat, Harold makes the introductions. "Al Babbit . . . Janice Jones and Heather Jacobs."

They exchange friendly smiles.

Harold adds, "Al's a distant cousin of mine from L.A."

Heather brightens. "I love L.A."

Babbit smiles. "Where are you from?"

Heather smiles back. "New York."

Babbit undoes the top two buttons on his long-sleeved cowboy shirt and spreads it open, revealing the writing below the red apple:

"I LOVE N.Y"

Heather turns to Janice. "I like this guy."

Everyone chuckles and Heather turns back to Babbit. "What is it that you do, Mr. Babbit?"

2

Babbit grins. "Do you mean what do I do to make a living?"

Janice laughs. "What she means is . . . are you a smart, fun, wealthy, highly-principled, Jewish bachelor?"

More chuckles ensue before Babbit answers, "Well, let me just say that I've been madly in love with the same girl that I first met on the day I flunked out of high school.

"And as to what I do to feed my family, my sweet little Irish mother, God bless her soul may she rest in peace . . . she always said the only thing I was ever properly trained to do was shoot dice. So, that's what I do for a living."

Heather smiles. "Sounds like fun."

Harold interjects, "Al's a movie producer. He just took a little break from Hollywood to spend a few days sailing around Elliot Bay, and now he's headed home. I'm giving him a ride to the airport. He's got a movie opening this weekend."

Heather gives Al a thumbs up. "Mind if I ask you something, Mr. Babbit?"

"Ask away."

"Could you tell me what it is that a producer does? His actual job?"

"How about if I tell you what my job 'should be' . . . according to the writers?"

Heather nods with a smile.

"They think that my job, once their so-called brilliant script has been put into my hands, is to buy it and get it filmed by a brilliant director–after first informing this brilliant director that the writer demands that he must shoot this brilliant script . . . scene by scene . . . word for word."

Heather chuckles.

Janice rolls her eyes and scoffs, "Writers."

Babbit continues, "The director believes that my job is to give him endless amounts of money and stay the hell out of his way . . . after first banning the writer from the set."

Heather and Janice are amused.

Babbit smiles. "And the actors? All they want from me is an Oscar role . . . and two boatloads of money."

The girls react: "Can't blame 'em for that."

Heather pursues the original question, "And what do you think a producer's job is?"

Babbit feigns a deep thought. "Our primary job, as I see it, is to not blow our brains out as we're dealing with these people."

Heather chuckles then strikes a more serious note. "What about 'after' you've actually found that brilliant script? Seriously."

Babbit puts the answer in a serious nutshell. "Make the absolute best movie possible . . . for the absolute least possible amount of money."

Everyone chuckles at the plain truth of the answer.

Heather smiles. "I love talking about movies. So, what's your movie about?"

"It's an old-fashioned kind of love story."

Heather needs more explanation. "Which is?"

"Boy meets girl, boy loses girl, boy gets girl back, and they ride off into the sunset to have a fabulous life together . . . if only . . ."

Heather doesn't hesitate, "If only what?"

Babbit lights a cigar, then closes the subject. "If only they both value love above everything else."

Heather is satisfied. "Been a long time since I've seen one of those."

Babbit nods. "I hope you and Janice will go see it . . . and take Harold with you."

Harold grins. "I dunno about that. It sure sounds like a chick-flick to me."

Janice reacts. "Oh really? And what exactly would make it a 'chick-flick?'"

Harold smirks. "Talk, talk, talkedy friggin' talk."

Heather chuckles, and Janice changes the subject, "Back to reality. Any prospects yet for the Swanky Shampane champagne commercial?"

Harold shrugs. "Possibly."

Janice is interested. "The guy from MTV?"

Harold nods. "Yeah. He's never directed a commercial before, but he definitely knows how to hold your attention for twenty seconds.

"He's a pothead, temporarily unemployed, mother's sick– he needs money. I think we can get him for peanuts."

Janice gives Harold a stern look, and he backs off. "All

right, all right, we'll pay him scale. I'm gonna meet with him in Chicago tomorrow morning."

"You already tell him what we're looking for?"

"I told him to quit toking and warm up the cameras when his brain drifts into that area between Dunkin' Donuts and 'Where's the beef?'

"Anyway, from there, I'll fly directly to Tahoe. What's your schedule?"

Janice is excited about their holiday together. "My flight gets into Reno at 7:30. I'll have breakfast there, then it's just a short drive up to Tahoe.

"I've rented a sexy little red sports car to match my latest little Victoria's Secret, just in case we decide to take a moonlight drive and park in the woods."

Harold chuckles. "Sounds like I might wanna slap on an extra dose of my Amani juice."

Janice responds with a lecherous lilt, "I would if I were you."

Harold now makes a point of reminding her, "Don't forget . . . it's only two more days until your New Year's resolution."

She reassures him, "I haven't forgotten. I'm already on my last pack."

"Okay, see you at Tahoe."

Everyone waves their "Glad to meetchas," and the group heads off in their respective directions.

After traveling less than twenty feet, Harold remembers something, stops, and backs up. "Janice! Wait a second!"

Janice turns back and again jogs in place.

Harold has news: "Did you happen to hear about your ex 'stud muffin'?"

Apparently, she hasn't. "What about him?"

"You didn't hear?"

"No. What happened?"

Harold overflows with self-righteousness, "He lost the Grampers account."

"No!"

"Oh yeah. Forty million a year. Gone!"

"What happened?"

"That's the best part, the way it happened. It seems that, while Mr. Perfect was spending the past year working out a new ten-year contract with the Grampers' lawyers, the owner of the company–the only one with the authority to sign a contract that size–took a little vacation.

"And nobody knows where he is or how to get ahold of him."

Janice is stunned. "Ricky has a forty-million-dollar unsigned contract?"

Harold beams with happiness. "You got it! Can you imagine the moment when Ricky Roy, the incredible Mr. Groovy, first got the news?"

"Can't they track the guy down?"

"No. He just disappeared. Left a note that said the world was going to hell, and he was sick and tired of all the bullshit."

"Wow."

"And now they've just found out that before he left, he gave his entire fortune to some inner-city youth program. All of it. Millions. Evidently, the guy is just goofier than shit."

"Wow."

"Yeah, Ricky Roy, Mr. Brilliant, getting dumped on by Grampers, the 'Pampers for old people.' Yes, there is a god."

"Harold, give it a rest, will you?"

"Sorry. The guy just pushes my buttons." Harold then grumbles something about an asshole, yanks the Mercedes into gear, and starts off, saying that he'll see Janice at Tahoe.

Janice waves goodbye, and once again, the girls jog off.

Harold steals a quick backward glance at Heather's departing butt and snarls back over his shoulder to Babbit, "You ought to see this guy Ricky Roy. Can you believe that for a fuckin' name? Ricky . . . Roy! What a fuckin' jerk."

CHAPTER TWO

In a quaint neighborhood several blocks from the ocean, Janice, carrying a large Macy's shopping bag full of boxes, pushes open a front gate.

In the living room, a computer, an ashtray, and a cat's food bowl sit on top of a large, inexpensive desk. There is also a cheap desk chair, a full-length mirror, a tattered sofa, an old television set, and a cat snoozing in a basket. And, most conspicuously, there are two wall-to-wall clothing bars loaded with expensive apparel.

Janice enters. She drops the Macy's bag onto the sofa, plops a handful of mail and a newspaper onto the desk, lights a cigarette, turns on FOX news, and walks into the kitchen.

She snaps on the light, opens a can of pork and beans, dumps it into a pot, and turns on a burner. She then proceeds to the bathroom, washes her face, puts on a baggy T-shirt, returns to the living room, caresses her cat, picks up the newspaper, and walks back into the kitchen.

She checks the food's temperature with her finger, takes a conspicuously ornate saltshaker, and sprinkles a dash of salt into the pot.

She then unfolds the newspaper and fastens it to a clip hanging on a string from a light fixture in the middle of the ceiling.

Now, with the newspaper's financial section open at eye level, Janice chops onions and hot dogs, smokes a cigarette, and reads.

Dinner is soon ready. She adds the onions and hot dogs to the pot, unclips the newspaper, snaps the light off, and walks back into the living room.

She scoops a helping of pork and beans into the cat's bowl and clips the newspaper onto another string hanging from a ceiling fixture.

She is now ready to multi-task: eat, smoke, read, watch the news, and peruse the mail as she opens the boxes from the Macy's bag.

Janice moves with robotic efficiency.

She puts a spoonful of pork and beans in her mouth and opens a piece of mail. Then she opens the first box. It contains red ski pants, and she holds them to her waist in front of the mirror. Next, she checks the stock market numbers on the newspaper's financial page as she smokes.

She then takes another mouthful of food and opens the next box. It's a red ski jacket, and she poses with it from several different angles in front of the mirror. Following that, she reads, eats, and opens another box. It contains a pair of red after-ski boots.

She continues along, taking another bite of food, smoking, and trying on a pair of red mittens and a red knit hat from the next box. She then unclips the newspaper, turns a page, reclips the newspaper, reads more numbers, and continues smoking while enjoying another mouthful of pork and beans.

Finally, she opens the last box and carefully removes a red negligee, holds it against her body, and poses in front of the mirror–while still wearing the mittens and the hat, and still with a cigarette dangling from her lips. (Charming, but not exactly the right accessory for a haute couture image.)

CHAPTER THREE

The following morning, Heather drives up in a slightly dented 1958 Chevy Impala, toots her horn, and parks. Janice walks out her front door holding a pet-cage with her cat inside, a carry-all bag slung over her shoulder, and pulling a large piece of luggage.

They load up the car and drive away.

At the first intersection, a street sign with the outline of an airplane and the letters SEA directs them toward the airport.

Their voices emanate from inside the car as it makes its way through traffic.

As Janice lights a cigarette, Heather remarks, "What a beautiful morning it is to be flying off for a New Year's holiday of skiing, dining, dancing, drinking, and having wild sex with the most ambitious and possibly the most handsome man in the entire advertising business.

"Life doesn't get much better than that."

Janice voices her concerns, "Do you think my breasts are too small?"

Heather voices her preferred subjet, "By the way, did I happen to mention that my uncle Bert died when he was only forty-six?"

Janice gives her a look as the car eases slowly through an intersection: *'Oh geez, not this again.'* She then replies aloud, "Are you referring to your uncle Bert who died a painfully slow and agonizing death from lung cancer, leaving your aunt Ruth alone to raise three precious little children?

"Yes, I think you did happen to mention it several thousand times."

Heather can be relentless. "Cigarettes also cause wrinkles on your face and make your breath stink."

Janice looks at her friend and pats her head as they pull up to a stoplight. "Like I told you yesterday, I'm on my last pack. I've smoked ten, I've got ten more to go, and that'll be the end of it. Done. Finished. And once again, I will be a healthy person. Okay?"

Heather persists, "I hear that quitting smoking is really hard to do."

Janice drops her chin onto her chest in exasperation as the light turns green and they pull away.

Heather makes an 'innocent' observation. "They say that even after you've quit, even years later, you'll still get urges to smoke."

Janice covers her ears.

Heather adds a little pessimistic reality into the mix, "Like if you smell the smoke from someone else's cigarette, you'll get a craving for one yourself."

Janice opens her window.

Heather has Janice 'on the ropes' and suggests the likelihood of failure, "I've also heard that once it's on your mind, even the smell of coffee could trigger an irresistible urge to . . ."

Janice hangs her head out the window to get away from Heather's voice.

* * *

Minutes later. Traffic has stalled. The radio clock reads 5:15.

Heather is curious, "Janice, can I ask you something?"

Janice responds, "Is it about smoking?"

"No."

Janice pulls her head back inside. "Okay, go ahead."

"How is it that you've got at least fifty thousand dollars worth of exquisite clothing . . . and yet you don't have twenty dollars worth of decent furniture?"

Janice smiles. "Wait until next year when I get my place on Skyline Drive. I'm gonna have a big house-warming party.

"And then you'll see a Thermador kitchen, Pizon bath towels, Rose Tarlow furniture, Richard Capel rugs, Menlo Park chandeliers, and right there . . . spread out across my Perigold bed . . . gramma's West Virginia State Fair, prize-winning, blue-ribbon quilt.

"And we'll all be drinking Swanky Shampane Champagne out of Swarovski Crystal."

Heather chuckles. Traffic starts to move. "And you're gonna feel comfortable living like that?"

Janice smiles, "Like a rat in a drainpipe."

Heather bursts a laugh and shakes her head.

CHAPTER FOUR

It's early morning in the mountains, and the snowpack is heavy. Icicles hang from the roof of a secluded two-story cabin situated in front of a high wall of boulders. It is starkly quiet.

Suddenly, Jeffrey, a bearded man in his mid-thirties, somersaults out of a second-story hayloft doorway. He lands on the rooftop of an old, beat-up blue pickup truck with one yellow and one red door. He bounces awkwardly onto the hood, slides to the ground, jumps into the idling truck, 'spins a doughnut' in the snow, and tears off down the snowy mountain road, past a road sign warning: DANGER. CLIFF AREA. KEEP OUT.

The truck turns onto a narrow, twisting, two-lane mountain highway and maintains its speed until it reaches a flashing road sign: STORM WARNING. SPEED LIMIT 25 M.P.H.

The truck's wheels lock up, sending it into a controlled slide and reducing its speed to the legal limit. A light snow begins

CHAPTER FOUR

falling. Around the next curve, a highway patrol officer sits in
a large four-by-four SUV with fully chained tires.

Jeffrey and the officer exchange friendly waves.

The truck travels through several more turns before coming
upon a little red convertible sports car stuck in a snow bank.
A woman in a beautiful red ski outfit stands alongside the car
in obvious need of help.

Jeffrey drives past her, muttering to himself, "Tourists."

Several minutes later, at the base of the mountain, Jeffrey
stops his truck next to a mailbox. He rolls down the window
and reaches out to get his mail. Jeffrey tosses the junk mail onto
the floor and slips the bills into his coat pocket. He then finds
the envelope he's been looking for, opens it, reads the contents,
crumbles it up, and tosses it onto the floor, grumbling, "Idiots
and imbeciles!"

He then makes a U-turn and heads back up the mountain.

* * *

Janice stands next to her car, fuming.

Jeffrey's pickup truck soon rattles back into the scene.

Janice marches out to the middle of the road and puts her
hands on her hips, daring him not to stop.

Jeffrey drives slowly around her and continues up the road.
Before long he glances into his rear-view mirror: Janice has one
hand on her hip, and the other threatens him with her fist.

17

Jeffrey mumbles to himself, "I pity the poor guy who has to sleep with that woman."

A short distance later, Jeffrey shrugs, stops, and backs up. "I must be nuts."

The truck rolls to a stop in front of the car. Jeffrey steps out, pulls the seat forward, and withdraws a tow rope. He walks to the car, hooks one end of the rope to the car frame, attaches the other end to his truck, and instructs Janice, "Get in your car, start the engine, and put it in neutral."

Janice hesitates, and Jeffrey clarifies his instructions: "Do you suppose you could start your engine and move that little dealie-bob to where it points to the little letter 'N'?"

Janice narrows her eyes and gets into her car as Jeffrey climbs into his truck.

Janice grumbles to her cat, who is curled up on the bucket seat next to her, "This man should have been eaten at birth."

The truck easily pulls the little car out of the snowbank.

Jeffrey backs up into the deep powder to slacken the tow rope. Leaving the engine running, he steps out of the truck, unhooks the rope from both vehicles, and gives Janice a little advice, "In the future, you might want to consider paying a little more attention to the road signs."

Janice smiles. "You might want to consider buying a cowbell and joining a jug band." She then gives him a little 'bye bye' wave and heads up the highway.

Jeffrey is disgusted by her attitude. But without wasting any more time, he stows the coiled rope, jumps into his truck, steps on the gas pedal–only to hear the sickening whirr of a tire that can't get traction, and with each acceleration, it grinds deeper into the sloping embankment. Jeffrey jumps out of his truck, evaluates the situation, and kicks a tire.

The lightly falling snow has increased in size and strength.

Traveling up the highway, Janice adjusts herself comfortably into the bucket seat, looks into the rear-view mirror to brush her eyebrows with a moistened fingertip, and sees Jeffrey giving his tire another kick.

Janice finishes preening and turns on the radio.

A few turns later, she comes upon the heavily chained highway patrol vehicle, which now blocks the road.

Janice stops her car, and the officer approaches. "Sorry ma'am, this is as far as you can go without chains or four-wheel drive."

"But my fiancé is already up at Sky Tavern waiting for me, can't I just–"

"Sorry. Chains or four-wheel drive. Big storm coming in."

"But officer, I just drove all the way from Wyoming, twenty-seven straight hours. We have reservations for the weekend–"

"Sorry."

Janice pouts, "But officer, my fiancé is in the military. I haven't seen him in a year. It's only a few more miles, can't I just–"

"Sorry."

"But—"

"No."

The officer steps back and indicates for her to make a U-turn and go back down the mountain. Janice, in a huff, turns her car around and zooms off.

Jeffrey is exasperated and ready to vent when he spots the little red car coming back down the mountain. He stomps over to the center of the road and folds his arms defiantly across his chest.

Janice pulls up and rolls down her window.

Jeffrey has an attitude. "Nice of you to come back. Conscience start bothering you?"

Janice acts innocent. "You're stuck? I didn't think trucks with four-wheel drive could get stuck. You do have four-wheel drive, don't you?"

"Of course I do."

"And once you get unstuck, you are going up the highway, aren't you?"

"Yes I am. That's why my truck is pointed in that direction."

Stifling her retort, Janice parks and gets out of her car.

Jeffrey tells her exactly what to do. "You get in the truck, put it in second gear, and when I give you the signal, press slowly on the gas pedal."

Janice climbs into the truck, rolls down the window, and puts it in second gear while Jeffrey methodically positions himself behind the truck, ready to push. "Okay!"

Janice punches it.

The tires spit bullets of snow back into Jeffrey's face, knocking him onto his butt. "I said slowly! You . . . dope!"

Janice thrusts her head out the window. "Don't you dare speak to me that way!"

Jeffrey wipes gobs of dirty, wet snow off his face and snarls under his breath.

Following that, and still separated by a safe distance, Jeffrey and Janice continue to scream at each other as each attempt to dislodge the truck fails. The music coming from the radio in Janice's vehicle is a heartbreaking rendition of Roberta Flack singing, "The First Time Ever I Saw Your Face."

CHAPTER FIVE

The snowfall has gotten noticeably thicker by the time they are finally underway, and with the cat and a small carry-all bag wedged between them, Jeffrey and Janice sit in hateful silence. Jeffrey looks sweaty and battered, and Janice couldn't possibly look more disgusted.

They travel this way for a distance, pass around the highway patrol roadblock, and before long, turn off the highway. Jeffrey stops the truck and looks over at Janice.

She speaks, "Why did you turn off the highway?"

"Because my cabin is down this road, off the highway."

"Well, I don't want to go to your cabin. I want to go to the Sky Tavern Ski Lodge."

"You could walk. Might even help you lose a few pounds." Janice gives him a piercing look, and he continues, "And besides, I don't have enough gas to get you there."

"Well, can't you get some? Guys like you always have a can of gasoline lying around someplace, don't you? I'll pay for it."

Jeffrey absorbs her comment then informs her of a simple fact: "Listen carefully, because I'm only going to say it one more time. I do not, have enough gas, to drive you, up, to Sky Tavern."

Janice looks at the gas gauge. The red arrow points exactly to the black line marking half a tank.

Janice now informs him of this seemingly relevant fact, "Your gas gauge says you've got half a tank."

Jeffrey sighs. "That is because I personally rigged the gauge to read half a tank, when, in fact, it's less than a mile away from being bone dry."

"And may I ask . . . why you did this?"

Animating his exasperation, Jeffrey decides on an answer. "Because life was getting just a little too predictable."

Janice forces a gob of irony through her disgust. "Interesting. And since you refuse to give me a ride up the mountain, do you suppose I could use the phone in your cabin?"

"Local call?"

"Very."

Jeffrey sighs and drives off toward his cabin, once again passing the sign: DANGER. CLIFF AREA. KEEP OUT.

CHAPTER SIX

Jeffrey crosses a cozy living room in his cabin where an old Basset hound sleeps between an unlit Christmas tree and a telescope on a tripod. There is also a small black and white television set, a rocking chair, a sofa, a bookcase, a barstool, a flight of stairs that lead up to a landing in front of a loft area, and a shoulder-high stack of firewood extending inward from the front door.

Jeffrey walks into the kitchen through a wide-open archway that has an old baseball mitt nailed above it.

Holding her cat and her carry-all bag, Janice enters and looks around. Pictures of cowboy movie stars are everywhere: from Roy Rogers and Hopalong Cassidy to John Wayne and Clint Eastwood.

In the kitchen, Jeffrey shakes a little instant-coffee into a cup, pours in a splash of milk, and adds hot tap water.

Janice sets her cat down and watches her meander over and lay down next to Jeffrey's dog.

Jeffrey walks out of the kitchen, takes off his winter garb, and gracefully tosses each item to its 'proper place.' (Gloves onto mantle, coat onto wall hook, and boots into a wooden box.) But the heavy knit hat remains on his head.

Janice patiently endures the ritual before speaking, "You do have a phone?"

Jeffrey retrieves an old rotary-style telephone from inside a closed trunk. "This is America. Everybody has a television, a toilet, at least one crappy relative with money, and a telephone."

Janice takes the phone. "Thank you."

Jeffrey heads upstairs to the loft, which is made private by the closing of two heavy curtains. "I'm going to work now. Please shut the door tightly on your way out."

Jeffrey then disappears through the curtains.

Janice pulls a vacation brochure from her coat and dials the number written across the beautiful alpine scenery on its cover.

The front-desk operator answers, "Sky Tavern Ski Lodge."

Janice speaks, "Harold Benson's room, please."

The connection is made. "Hello."

"Hello darling, it's me."

Harold asks, "Janice, where are you?"

"My car got stuck on the highway, some hillbilly drove me to his cabin, and . . . just come and get me. I'll tell you all about it when you get here. And have the hotel send a tow truck down to pick up my car. My luggage is still in the trunk, and the car is just off the road a couple of miles or so below Sky Tavern."

"Okay. I'll send somebody down to get you right away. What's the phone number where you're at?"

Janice reads the number from the phone, "555-1553."

"And the address?"

"Hang on." Janice raises her voice to reach the loft, "Excuse me." But there is no answer, so she raises her voice even more, "Excuse me!"

Jeffrey appears through the curtain. "What?"

Janice indicates towards the road. "What do you call this road?"

Jeffrey answers, "Boo Boo Magoo."

Janice makes certain she heard correctly, "Boo, Boo, Magoo?"

Jeffrey tolerates her deafness, "That's right. Boo Boo Magoo."

"Thank you." She then repeats into the phone what she heard as Jeffrey exits back through the curtains. "Boo Boo Magoo."

"Got it. Boo Boo Magoo. What's the street address?"

"Harold, it doesn't matter. You can't miss it. It's the dumpy-looking place in front of a big rock-pile, with an old beat-up truck parked in front of it."

"Okay, I'll get someone down there right away."

"Please hurry." Janice smacks a kiss into the phone and hangs up.

Janice looks around, sighs in disgust, and once again calls up to the loft, "Excuse me." She waits for a response, gets none, so tries again, louder, "Excuse me!"

Jeffrey comes back through the curtains. "Now what?"

"Do you mind if my cat and I stay inside until my ride comes?"

"No, I don't mind. Do you mind if I get back to work without any further interruptions?"

Janice indicates with her hand: "Be my guest."

Jeffrey fakes a smile. "Thank you." And exits back through the curtains.

Janice brushes off a sofa cushion and sits down. Seconds pass, and the phone rings. She lets it ring twice and is about to answer it when Jeffrey emerges through the curtains, hurries down the stairs, and answers it himself. "Jeffrey Brown speaking."

Harold speaks, "Hello, is Janice Jones there, please?"

Jeffrey can't believe what is happening to his day. He lowers the phone and turns to Janice. "I believe it's for you."

Janice looks slightly apologetic.

Jeffrey hands her the phone. "By the way, this happens to be a business phone."

Janice takes the phone. "My apologies."

Jeffrey exaggerates a smile and heads back up to the loft.

Janice waits for Jeffrey to get out of hearing range before putting the phone to her ear. "Hello?"

Harold responds. "Janice, I just spoke with the limousine

service and the front desk. And nobody has ever heard of Boo Boo Magoo Road."

Janice reacts, "Good God Almighty!"

Jeffrey has already disappeared through the curtains when once again Janice calls loudly up to him, "Excuse me."

Jeffrey reappears. His mood is now similar to Janice's. "What?"

"Did you or did you not say this road outside was Boo Boo Magoo Road?"

"I did not. You asked me what I call it. I call it the Boo Boo Magoo Road. It doesn't have an official name. So that is why I call it what I want to call it.

"I named it after the two individuals I admire most. Boo Boo, the short smart bear from the Huckleberry Hound Show, and Mr. Magoo, the guy who can't see anything but has good luck and a big nose.

"Hence the name, Boo Boo Magoo."

Janice, stunned in disbelief, raises the phone back to her ear. "Harold, get me out of here."

Harold responds, "Janice, ask this person where his cabin is in relation to Sky Tavern."

Janice turns her attention back to Jeffrey. "Where, exactly, are we, in relation to Sky Tavern?"

"Tell them to drive three miles down the Mt. Rose Highway, take a right on the only road available, continue on for five hundred yards, and stop at the baby blue pickup truck.

"And be sure to remind them . . . the sooner, the better."

Jeffrey disappears back through the curtains.

Janice now whispers back into the phone. "Harold, we are not dealing with your average run-of-the-mill idiot here. This man is world-class. So, listen carefully, and please hurry. Drive three miles . . ."

CHAPTER SEVEN

Outside, the storm has intensified. Holding her cat, Janice paces around the front porch, waiting for her ride.

Inside, the phone rings. Janice stops pacing and listens. It rings again. She hesitates at the front door. It rings again. She opens the door slightly and sticks an ear inside.

Jeffrey comes quickly down the stairs and answers the phone. "Jeffrey Brown speaking."

Janice now sticks her entire head inside. Jeffrey notices. The caller speaks. "Janice Jones, please."

Jeffrey responds, "Certainly, let me see if she's available at the moment." Jeffrey covers the mouthpiece and whispers loudly to Janice. "Are you free to take a call?"

Janice gives him a look and enters the cabin.

Jeffrey speaks politely into the phone. "She'll be with you momentarily."

Janice takes the phone, and Jeffrey smiles, but she's going to wait for him to leave the room so she can speak privately. He understands. "I'll just go into the kitchen so that you can have some privacy."

"Thank you." Janice now speaks quietly into the phone, "Harold?"

"Janice, it's storming like hell up here. They're plowing the road now. They say it'll be a couple of hours before anyone can get through."

"Harold, I'm in a cabin with a man who has no brain. This man could murder me and plead insanity, and nobody would question it. The man's role model is Mr. Magoo. Harold, get me out of here."

"Janice, please, get ahold of yourself. We'll get down there as soon as possible. Until then, just humor the man, and everything will be fine."

"I suppose. But, please hurry."

Janice hangs up and rubs her hands together to warm them. It probably hasn't occurred to Jeffrey just how cold the cabin is since he still wears two sweaters and a heavy knit hat.

Jeffrey walks out of the kitchen sipping a fresh cup of coffee, and Janice attempts to put their circumstances in a new perspective. "Mr. Brown. Should I call you Mr. Brown?"

"Yes."

"Fine. Now, Mr. Brown, I have nowhere to go. The highway

THE NEW YEAR'S RESOLUTION

is closed. The plows are working on it. And it'll be a couple of hours before my fiancé can get down here to rescue me.

"I would like to give you twenty dollars and rent the use of your cabin for a couple of hours."

Jeffery considers their situation, "Since we seem to have no other choice, I suppose, under certain conditions, I could tolerate your presence for a couple of hours."

"You have a fascinating way with words, Mr. Brown."

"As do you, Miss Jones, or is it . . . Ms. Jones?"

"You may call me Janice. May I call you Jeffrey?"

"No, I prefer that you call me Mr. Brown."

"Fine, and what are the conditions under which you think you may be able to tolerate my presence?"

"Do not whine for any reason whatsoever." Then, indicating to a large red button at the top of the stairs, Jeffrey adds, "And do not ask any dumb questions like . . . 'What's that button for?' Or, 'How do you build a fire?'"

Janice takes a checkbook and a pen out of her purse. "Fine. I believe I can function under those conditions. Now, if you'll be good enough to tell me the proper spelling of your last name, I shall write you a check."

Janice sits on the sofa to write the check and looks up at Jeffrey to get the proper spelling.

Jeffrey feigns difficulty with the spelling of his last name. "B. R. O. W. –"

Janice seems a little irritated. "I hope you didn't find

32

my question too dumb, Mr. Brown, but as you know, Brown is sometimes spelled with an 'E' on the end, as in Theodore Browne, the conductor of the London Philharmonic Symphony Orchestra, or B. R. A. U. N. as it is spelled by the Chancellor of Austria, Frederick von Braun."

Jeffrey answers politely, "Of course."

Janice writes the check and hands it to Jeffrey. He looks it over. "Do you have any identification?"

"Credit card suffice?"

"Anything with your picture on it?"

Janice takes the driver's license out of her wallet.

Jeffrey takes the license and scrutinizes it. "It says here that you were born the same year as me." He then looks at Janice's face. "Hmm. You look older than that."

Janice holds her tongue. Jeffrey hands back the license, puts the check in his pocket, and speaks as he heads back to the loft, "If you're cold, build a fire."

Shivering from the cold, Janice sets her cat on an old barstool near the stack of firewood. A box of newspapers is close by, as is a tree stump with an axe whacked into it. The cat jumps off the barstool and again curls up next to the dog as Janice takes a newspaper, wads up a few pages, and tosses them into the fireplace. She then sets a log onto the middle of the paper, takes a cigarette lighter from her purse, lights a corner of one page, and stands back to bask in the warmth of a blazing fire.

Within moments, smoke is pouring into the living room. Jeffrey calls out from behind the loft's curtains. "Open the damper, Janice."

Janice opens the damper, though by now, all the paper is burned up, and the log is only slightly scorched. She then wads up a mound of newspaper pages, places the scorched log on top of it, and sets the mound on fire. This time the smoke does go up the chimney. Unfortunately, the blazing fire lasts only as long as it takes the paper to burn, and Janice is once again left standing in front of a scorched log amid flaky ashes. She casts a glance up to the loft.

Jeffrey stands at the top of the stairs, throbbing with superiority. He then skips down the stairs, positions the scorched log on the stump, and chops kindling with ease.

Then he arranges the kindling in the fireplace, crisscrosses four logs on top of it, tears off one small strip of newspaper, lights it, sets it under the kindling . . . and begins what will soon become a roaring fire.

As the fire builds, Jeffrey takes the whisk broom hanging from the mantle and sweeps his small mess into a tiny mound, which he then pinches between two fingers and drops into the fire.

Jeffrey turns to Janice, who has been watching all this, and asks, "Would you care to attempt making yourself a cup of coffee? It's instant."

Janice follows Jeffrey across the room and speaks as he

bounds happily back up the stairs, "Just for your information, I happen to have a master's degree in marketing from Stanford University."

Jeffrey pauses at the landing before disappearing through the curtains. "Wonderful. Maybe sometime I'll see you at the market . . . and you can help me pick out my vegetables."

Janice loosens her coat as she speaks to Jeffrey's dog. "You poor dear thing. You could have done so much better."

Janice pulls two and one-half bent and soggy cigarettes from a badly damaged pack inside her coat pocket. She then spreads them out to dry near the fire, lovingly rotating them as the side nearest the flames becomes dry.

Once the half-cigarette is fully dry, Janice lights it up and– savoring every moment while discreetly blowing the smoke into the fireplace–smokes it down to a quarter of an inch before pinching out the tiny butt and tucking it back into her shirt pocket for safekeeping. She then wraps the other two cigarettes in a Kleenex tissue, buttons them into her other shirt pocket, and sits in the rocking chair to await her rescue.

A few moments pass before Jeffrey bolts from the loft, scurries down the stairs, darts past Janice's rocking chair, and arrives at the bookcase. He quickly reaches behind a particular book, searches, comes up empty, tries behind another book, again comes up empty. He then picks up the barstool, places it against the large front window, climbs it, and reaches up for the vase sitting on top of the valance.

He checks the vase for contents. It's empty. He climbs back down, returns the barstool to its place next to the stack of firewood, and hurries back past the rocking chair and up the stairs.

(This strange activity is familiar to all who have ever given up smoking: the search for that one cigarette that was once, long ago, hidden away in case of an emergency.)

Janice reacts to all this without speaking: "This guy is nuttier than a fruitcake."

CHAPTER EIGHT

In his comfy room in the lodge at Sky Tavern, Harold unpacks his luggage and hangs the clothes in the closet. The door is ajar, and a most eligible snow bunny–over eighteen and blonde–soon sticks her head inside. "Hello."

Harold is pleasantly surprised. "Hello to you."

She smiles. "I hope I'm not bothering you. My friend and I are just across the hall, and we saw you arrive, so we thought we'd be neighborly and invite you to join us for a drink."

Harold glances at his watch and quickly calculates. "I'd love to. Let me finish hanging these clothes."

"Cool. We'll wait for you in the lounge."

She leaves, her butt rolling deliciously under the clinical scrutiny of Harold's eyes.

Minutes later, as the blonde and her friend, a beautiful

redhead, sip drinks at a private table overlooking Lake Tahoe, Harold approaches.

The blonde smiles and comments, "That was fast."

Harold smiles back. "I'm a fast guy."

"Not in everything you do, I hope."

The redhead playfully slaps at the blonde's hand. "You're so bad."

Harold introduces himself and shakes hands with the girls. "Derek Darnell."

The blonde responds, "Nice to meet you, Derek. I'm Holly, and this is my friend Molly."

Harold sits down as he motions for a cocktail girl. "Nice to make your acquaintance."

Holly pushes things along, "I hope our acquaintance is not all you want to make."

They all share a giggle as Molly rolls her eyes to acknowledge her friend's silly forwardness.

Harold inquires, "Where you girls from?"

Holly answers, "Yakima."

"Yakima, Washington?"

Holly nods. "Is there any other Yakima? Why do you ask?"

Harold smiles. "Frankly, my dear . . . I just like hearing you say Yakima."

They all chuckle, and Molly enters the conversation, "If you're going to call her your 'dear,' then I'm going to call you my 'daddy.'"

Harold laughs a 'whatever.' Then asks, "So, what do you girls do for work?"

Holly smiles. "I'm a sales rep for Dempsey Brothers Trucking. I handle all their northwest accounts."

Molly grins. "I handle all their other things."

Again, they all chuckle at the sexual innuendo as a cocktail waitress arrives to take their order. "What may I get you, sir?"

Harold replies, "How about a hot tub and a bowl of condoms."

The girls laugh. The waitress is not amused.

Harold acknowledges her mood. "Just kidding, just kidding." Then he orders the drinks, "Another round for the girls, and I'll have a vodka martini. Grey Goose."

The cocktail girl leaves. And Harold comments, "Kind of a sour puss, wasn't she?"

The girls nod in agreement, and Harold gets the chit-chat back on track. "So, how long are you ladies here for?"

Holly slips some relevant information into the conversation, "We've already been here a week. We're going home at noon tomorrow. Too bad you're just getting here. We'll probably never see you again after noon tomorrow."

Harold smiles.

CHAPTER NINE

Back in the living room at the cabin, Jeffrey is nowhere to be seen. He's up in the loft, working quietly behind the closed curtains.

Waiting for Harold, Janice sits in the rocking chair sipping coffee and maneuvering a long strand of dental floss between her two front teeth. Her cat is fast asleep, nestled peacefully with the dog. Janice soon drifts off into a recent memory of her ride to the airport with Heather: It's early morning, and the slightly dented Impala pulls up to an intersection where a street sign with the outline of an airplane and the letters SEA directs them to turn at the next corner. The radio clock reads 5:30.

Heather is speaking, "Do you want me to tell you something?"

Janice is curious. "Is it some secret that you promised not to tell?"

"Yes."

"Okay, tell me."

Heather has a single condition for releasing this information. "You promise not to tell?"

Janice has no problem accepting this stipulation. "Of course."

"Okay, listen to this. You know Judy Baker, the tall, red-headed girl from the Macy's sales department?"

"Your third best friend?"

Heather lowers her voice. "Yes. Well, listen to this . . . Wednesday afternoon she was feeling sick so she went home early, opened the door, and there, on the living room rug, her husband was doing it with another woman!"

"No!"

"Yes! Doggie-style!"

"Omigod! What did she do?"

"What could she do . . . she burst into tears and ran away."

Janice is appalled. "No!"

Heather shrugs. "What else could she do?"

Janice is defiant. "I would have calmly stood there and watched, and then I would have said to my husband, 'If you are now finished, you may now leave. And don't ever try to come back, because there are absolutely no circumstances under which I would ever take you back.'"

Heather is impressed. "You could do that?"

"No problem whatsoever."

Janice sticks her arm out the window to claim a space for Heather to access a faster lane as she reinforces her determination. "Why let some jerk put you through hell? When it's over, it's over. Period. Forget it. Put it behind you. Move on. What's the problem?"

The car stops at a red light.

Heather changes the subject, "You're so lucky. Just imagine, no crazy freeway drivers. No deranged street preachers. No crackhead gangbangers. No new-age goofballs. No big-city insanity for an entire week.

"Just mountains, and trees, and snow, and fresh air. Wow. One entire week without . . . weirdness!"

Suddenly, Jeffrey's raging voice breaks into Janice's memory: "Die! You scum-sucking swine!"

CHAPTER TEN

Janice goes stiff in the rocking chair. Her eyes widen, and her jaw drops. Silence follows. Her eyes move up to the narrow opening where Jeffrey hadn't quite pulled the loft's curtains tightly together.

Mustering her courage–and without realizing that the dental floss still hangs from her teeth–Janice sneaks slowly over to the bottom of the stairs, stops, listens, then creeps silently upwards.

Cautiously, she peeks over the top stair. She listens. Then, crawling on her belly, she inches her way across the landing toward the opening in the curtains. But just before she reaches a point where she will be able to peek through, Jeffrey emerges and is instantly past her as he scurries down the stairs.

Janice reacts: "Oh dear God."

Jeffrey moves swiftly across the living room to search the same two places in the bookcase that he had searched previously. Again, he comes up empty-handed. He sets the barstool in front of the window, climbs it, stretches up to reach the vase, turns it upside down, and shakes it. But it's still empty. He returns the barstool to its place next to the firewood, scampers back up the stairs, and is about to pass through the curtains–when he notices Janice.

She is now situated at the far end of the landing, standing on her head in front of a wooden hayloft-type door attached to a pulley rope.

Jeffrey is genuinely curious. "What . . . are you doing?"

Janice seems surprised by the question. "Nothing."

Jeffrey seems surprised by her seeming to be surprised. "Just standing on your head?"

Janice appears unconcerned. "It's yoga. I'm doing it up here because the carpet is softer than downstairs."

Janice unfolds out of the headstand and stands up.

Jeffrey informs her that, "It's the exact same carpeting."

Janice now proceeds nonchalantly along the landing and down the stairs, still unaware that a strand of dental floss dangles from her front teeth, bobbing with her every word as she declares, "I know it's the same. However, the carpet downstairs has been walked on more than the carpet upstairs, and so it's squished down more, and that's why it's not as soft. Obviously."

44

Jeffrey checks his wristwatch: "Isn't it two hours already?"

From the living room, Janice looks up at the loft. Jeffrey has departed back through the curtains, allowing her a chance to escape.

Keeping her eyes peeled on the loft, Janice picks up her cat and coat, quietly opens the front door, slides out, and runs off through the snow.

CHAPTER ELEVEN

Jeffrey sits at his desk. An old movie poster hangs on the wall featuring Elvis, with a six-shooter strapped to his hip, as he curls a lip and pulls a comb back through his hair.

Jeffrey moves to the center of the room, pauses, turns slowly back toward the desk, points a finger at his empty chair, and in a tortured display of melodramatic savagery . . . rages. "Die! You scum-sucking swine . . . of a devil!"

He then moves back to his desk, sits, and presumably writes down the additional words, ". . . of a devil!"

Satisfied, he smiles and lounges back to contemplate and gesture his way to his next choice of words. At last, he stands, moves back to the center of the room, takes a deep breath, once again points at his desk chair . . . and improves upon his dramatic prose. "Die! You scum-sucking swine, of a devil . . . whore pig!"

And, with an indication of being overwhelmed by the

brilliance of the additional words ". . . whore pig," he returns to his desk to enter the words in his writing tablet.

An alarm clock rings; it's 5:40. Jeffrey straightens the papers on his desk and walks out through the curtains.

Passing through the living room, Jeffrey turns the television to the local news, notices that Janice is gone, and mumbles in regard to her absence. "Goodbye, thank you for pulling my car out of the snow, thank you for letting me stay inside, thank you for not killing me as I was screwing up your entire morning. Thank you, thank you very much."

Jeffrey enters the kitchen, takes the dirty blender jar out of the sink, gives it a quick rinse, and attaches it back to the blender's base.

He then reaches into the hand-painted lime green refrigerator, extracts an egg, and places it carefully into his shirt pocket. Then he takes a banana, peels it, and breaks it into three sections to 'shoot' at the blender.

First, he misses a free throw from the full length of the kitchen, then, somehow, he misses a driving layup, then, dramatizing the event as he proceeds, he finally manages to score. "Brown, in the near court. He's double-teamed, eight seconds left in the game, Boston down by one. He fakes to the left, seven seconds, six, five, four.

"Brown is trapped on the baseline. Three men are on him. He fakes to the right. Three seconds left, two, Brown goes up . . ." Jeffrey now 'skyhooks' his last remaining section of banana.

47

"One second left. It's in the air! It's good! Brown has done it again! The fans are going crazy!

" Women are throwing their bras at him!"

Jeffrey jumps into the air and high-fives the baseball mitt nailed above the archway, thus ending speculation as to its actual purpose.

He then reaches into the cupboard, pulls out a handful of raisins and a handful of walnuts, and drops them into the blender. Then it's back into the refrigerator for yogurt, apple juice, pineapple juice, strawberry juice, prune juice, and a little pinch of cauliflower. Except for one last ingredient, the meal is ready to blend.

Jeffrey shakes out his arms, stretches out his back, rolls his neck, then climbs up onto the drainboard and stands, slightly stooped, directly above the blender. After several deep breaths, he takes the egg out of his pocket, concentrates, and– as confidently as can be– Jeffrey taps the egg against his forehead . . . sending the yoke falling straight down into the blender. "Bingo!"

Jeffrey jumps down from the drainboard, picks up his two missed banana-shots, scrapes them clean and drops them into the blender, flips the switch, and walks out of the kitchen a very happy guy.

Across the kitchen wall, outside the window where Janice, appearing nearly frozen to death, reacts to what she has just witnessed: "Oh . . . my . . . God!"

CHAPTER TWELVE

It's evening. In the lobby of the Sky Tavern Lodge, Harold converses with the chalet manager, a dignified man in his mid-sixties who is telling Harold about the latest storm conditions. "I'm quite certain that a limousine would not be able to make it down that road, but we could probably get a snowmobile in there without much trouble."

Harold offers his opinion, "Sounds dangerous."

The manager politely disagrees, "It's perfectly safe. Just a little noisy. Maybe a little bumpy."

Harold prefers a safer option. "I'd rather not have her out in the cold like that. I know it's silly, but I worry about her. I'd rather wait until we can send a nice warm limousine to pick her up."

The manager shrugs. "That might not be until tomorrow afternoon."

Harold has the last word, "Better safe than sorry."

* * *

Back at the cabin, Jeffrey turns up the volume on the local weather report. ". . . and that about wraps it up. The record low for this day of the year was in 1915 when the nighttime temperature fell to eighteen degrees below zero.

"We expect to break that record tonight. So please, if it's at all possible, bring your animals indoors."

Jeffrey pushes a well-worn cartridge into the VCR, and the weatherman is cut off by old black and white stock-footage featuring cowboys gunfighting, damsels being rescued, and horses rearing high up onto their back legs.

Jeffrey darts into the kitchen, turns off the blender, disconnects the jar, returns to the living room, and pours a hearty portion of his blended concoction into the dog's bowl. He then sits in front of the television and is immediately engrossed in the lives of his heroes: the men who brought righteousness, clean living, and justice to the American West.

Before long, the front door creaks as it opens, and the wind howls through. And, looking thoroughly punished from the subzero temperature, Janice enters the cabin, just as a voice sounding very much like Clint Eastwood comes from the television set. "You punks better get your names tattooed on your ass . . . just so the undertaker knows what to write on your tombstone."

Jeffrey presses the remote, stopping the action.

As Janice makes her way over to the fireplace, she pulls her cat from inside her coat and sits her on the woodpile.

Jeffrey asks, "Forget something? Like saying, 'Thank you, Jeffrey, for pulling my car out of the snowbank and providing me with the shelter of your home'?" He gets out of the rocking chair, puts the remote in his pocket, and, speaking baby talk, sympathizes with the cat. "Hey widdo guy, you must be fweezing."

He picks the cat up and heads for the kitchen. "You look skinny. Doesn't anybody ever feed you?"

Janice, her nose beet red and draining snot, mumbles weakly through her frozenness. "She eats twice a day. Chopped kidneys and sirloin tips."

"What did you say?"

Janice is too weak to raise her voice. "She eats twice a day. Chopped kidneys and sirloin tips."

Jeffrey leans out of the kitchen. "What?"

Janice mumbles, "Nothing. Nothing."

Jeffrey disappears back into the kitchen.

Before long, he returns to the living room, sets the cat and an empty bowl close to the fireplace, and pours the cat a heaping portion of blended dinner.

Janice looks at the strange food. "What is that?"

"That is a 'downtown Jeffrey Brown' power-shake. Guaranteed to put hair on your chest and lead in your pencil."

"You're a vegetarian?"

"That's right. Red meat makes me fart."

Janice forces a smile. "And your dog is a vegetarian?"

"That's right, makes him fart too."

Janice bends a little closer to the fireplace as a way to drop the subject.

Jeffrey gives the cat a friendly little head scrub. "What's the little guy's name, anyway?"

Janice appears to be annoyed by the question. "Erika."

Jeffrey playfully roughs up the cat. "Erika?! What the heck kind of name is that for a guy?"

"She's not a guy."

"Well, even for a girl, I mean c'mon. Erika? Where'd you get that name, from some soap opera celebrity?"

Janice ignores the question.

Jeffrey persists, "Is Erika her whole name, or is it Erika Danielle?" Jeffrey is quite pleased with himself at the moment, and now speaks with a French accent, "Or is it Erika Danielle . . . St. Deveraux."

Janice seems to resent Jeffrey's attitude. "What's your hound's name?"

Jeffrey stands and moves to the rocking chair. "My dog?"

"Yeah. That snoring mound of wrinkles."

Jeffrey answers in a soft voice, "Rambo."

Janice perks up. "I beg your pardon?"

Jeffrey repeats himself with his voice slightly elevated. "Rambo."

Janice is aroused by the direction this conversation seems to be going, "Rambo?"

"That's right."

Janice responds, with a Bronx accent, "Is dat Rambo period? Or is dat Rambo Rocky? Or, is dat Rambo Rocky da ramblin' man? Or is dat–"

Jeffrey isn't amused. "Ya know, you seem to have a little problem with manners, Janice."

Janice is even more energized by this latest exchange. "Really?"

"That's right. You don't walk into a person's home and immediately start disrespecting his dog."

"You were disrespecting my cat."

"No, I wasn't. I was kidding good-naturedly about your cat with no malice intended, and you took offense because of some basic insecurity in your own personality. And in your attempt to overcome this inferiority complex, you ridiculed my dog."

"No, I didn't."

"Yes, you did."

"I certainly did not."

"You absolutely did."

"Did not."

"Did."

Janice smiles. "Why don't we just forget it?"

Jeffrey smiles back. "That's fine with me. I couldn't care less."

"Okay then, we'll just forget it."

"Fine." Jeffrey starts rocking his chair, angrily.

Janice returns to the problem at hand. "May I borrow your phone, please?"

"Why not–you've borrowed it three times already."

Janice dials. Jeffrey clicks the videotape back into action.

Janice attempts to reach her party over the loud gunfighting. "Harold Benson's room, please."

After a hateful glance towards Jeffrey, who is still vigorously rocking and silently fuming in his chair, Janice raises her voice, "Excuse me, Mr. Brown, but I wonder if I might impose upon you to turn the sound down just a teensy bit?"

"Why don't I just turn it completely off?"

"I don't think that'll be necessary, Mr. Brown."

Jeffrey presses the remote button that again freeze-frames the brawling cowboys. "But it's my house, and I insist."

Janice forces a smile. "Thank you." Then continues with her call to Harold, "Hello, Harold? This is Janice. I am calling to find out exactly when you will be here."

CHAPTER THIRTEEN

Up at the lodge, wearing a fluffy designer robe, Harold stands at the washbasin leaning close to the mirror, clipping his nose-hairs with a small pair of scissors. The receiver from a phone is situated on the sink to accommodate his call from Janice.

"Hello darling, I just this moment found out the road is totally closed. The plows can't possibly get through until probably around noon tomorrow.

"And as lousy as it sounds, we're just gonna have to accept it. We have no other choice. I'm sure the gentleman there at the cabin will understand our predicament and offer you his guest room for the night."

"Perfect."

"But, I'll be there when the first plow is allowed through. You can count on that."

"Well then, toodle-do."

* * *

Jeffrey has heard Janice's end of her conversation with Harold and hopes to learn that the plows are only minutes away. "Good news, Janice?"

Janice moves back to the warmth of the fireplace. "The road is closed, and the plows won't be able to get through until sometime around noon tomorrow."

"That is not good news."

"I am prepared to write you a check for one hundred dollars for the use of your home until that time."

Jeffrey gives it some thought, gets up out of the rocking chair, and motions for Janice to have a seat. With his hands clasped behind his back, he takes a thoughtful stroll around the perimeter of the hearth. "Janice, let me tell you a little something about myself.

"First of all, I've already got a hundred dollars. As a matter of fact, I've got over a thousand dollars.

"My cabin is totally paid for. I've got a well-stocked refrigerator, two cords of dry firewood, and four tubes of unopened toothpaste . . . econo-size.

"So, as you can see, I don't need your hundred dollars. The question is, do I want your hundred dollars? Is it worth a hundred dollars to have you here, on the premises, all night?

"Now, if you intend to act like my dog, to just hang around, not say anything, not cause any trouble, then yes, for a hundred dollars, it might be worth it.

"But if you intend to be an argumentative know-it-all with the manners of a radio talk show celebrity, then no, I'm afraid one hundred dollars wouldn't even begin to cover it."

Jeffrey leans back against the mantle. "So, before I decide whether or not I want your hundred dollars, I need to know which of those two things you intend to be."

Janice is momentarily dumbfounded by Jeffrey's insolence, but then she stands up and motions for him to sit down. It is now her turn to stroll around the hearth as he rocks in the chair. "Jeffrey, let me tell you a little something about myself.

"When I was eight years old, I led a small group of third-graders in a protest over an unfair playground policy that did not allow girls equal access to the school's one and only catcher's mask.

"When I was seventeen, I was the head cheerleader, president of my class, valedictorian, and voted most likely to rule the planet.

"Last month, I met with the Chairman of the Republican National Committee, at his urging, so that I might explain, in detail, my ideas on a media strategy for the next presidential campaign.

"So, as you may have guessed, just being here, alone with you, in a cabin, does not, in itself, constitute, the pinnacle of achievement . . . to which I personally aspire.

"I'm here because 'something' went horribly wrong."

Now Jeffrey is dumbfounded. He gets out of the rocking chair, motions for Janice to sit, and, once again, he territorializes the hearth while Janice rocks in the chair.

"If I turn you out into the cold, you will die, and it is remotely possible that some sort of misguided criminal charge could be brought against me.

"Now, at this particular time in my life, when I am in the process of monumentally important work, I dare not have my time interrupted by some long, drawn-out, totally irrelevant legal proceeding.

"So, it seems that I'm now confronted with a little problem. If I absolutely must allow you to spend the night here, how can I do so without hearing your voice?"

Jeffrey now pauses to think before continuing. "Maybe you could tape a mitten over your mouth?"

Without missing a beat, Janice replies, "Maybe you could stick it in your ear."

Jeffrey forces a smile. "That's an interesting expression. Is that going to be the new Republican campaign slogan?"

Janice gets out of the rocker and moves to the hearth. This overly bold move bothers Jeffrey immensely as he is determined to remain firmly established in this area.

Janice reclaims her dignity. "Listen, buster, there is no possible way for me to leave your cabin. One hundred dollars is more than a fair price for these . . . accommodations.

"Therefore, I intend to spend the night . . . without incident."

Jeffrey now re-establishes his position as lord and master of this abode. "Oh really? And just what would you do if I ordered you off my property?"

"I'd kick you in the groin and jam my fingernails into your eyeballs."

Jeffrey is horrified. "You'd what?"

"You heard me. I've been expertly trained in rape prevention, and I will use that training if and when I have to."

"Rape?! Are you out of your mind?! Do you realize how long I'd have to be without a woman before I'd want to have sex with you?!

"Try one lifetime! No, better make it two! Just in case!"

Janice responds, "Let's quit pussyfooting around. You sleep up the loft, and I'll sleep down here.

"Tomorrow, we won't even bother saying goodbye. We'll just pretend that we've never met–and hope that we never meet again."

Jeffrey leans back against the mantle. "That sounds perfect to me, Janice, except for one little thing."

Asserting his authority, Jeffrey takes a red candle off a nearby shelf and draws a wax line across the mantle's center. Then he bends down and continues the wax line across the center of the hearth. "By the way, Janice, don't cross that line, or I will throw your butt outta here. I don't care if it's three o'clock in the morning and fifty below zero."

He now saunters off the hearth and sits back down in the rocking chair. "Now, as I was saying, about your suggestion for our sleeping arrangements . . . it was perfect except for one little thing.

"The part about sleeping in separate places and not even having to say goodbye was perfect. That appealed to me immensely.

"However, the one thing you are apparently unaware of is that the 'up there' you spoke of . . . is my office . . . and nobody sleeps in my office. Not even me."

Janice reacts to the wax line, the physical threat, and the news about his sacred office: "I have a friend, that knows a guy, that had a monkey who defecated in his food bowl–every day– and then put the bowl on his head, upside down.

"And I honestly and truly believe that if that monkey were ever turned loose, his chances of leading a meaningful life . . . are infinitely better than yours."

CHAPTER FOURTEEN

Back at the lodge, in a very luxurious restaurant overlooking Lake Tahoe, Harold dines with Molly and Holly. Soft music plays in the background.

Molly touches Harold's hand. "I just love your name. Derek Darnell. It sounds so sexy. It's so rhythmic. Like Calvin Klein. Or Burt Bachrach."

Harold's inner voice says to himself: "I wouldn't mind having Burt's money."

Holly chimes in. "Or Danny DeVito?"

Again, Harold's voice is heard: "Wouldn't mind having his money either."

Molly has another good one, "How about Kevin Costner?"

Harold's inner voice reacts to this latest comparison, "Whatever."

Molly really enjoys this game. "How about Ozzy Osbourne?"

Harold's inner voice is losing interest, "How about enough already?"

Holly tracks back through the television programs that she watches. "George Jefferson! He cracks me up! 'Wha' chu' want Willis?!'"

Harold rolls his eyes and signals for the waiter as he changes the subject. "Tell you what . . . you can both just call me daddy, and we'll let it go at that."

The waiter arrives, and Harold, slipping him a fifty-dollar bill, attempts to repair the evening's damaged sexual tension. "What would be the chances of your finding us a bottle of Chateau LaFite, or something of that stature?"

Holly smiles at the waiter. "Daddy's a connoisseur."

The waiter pockets the dough, nods, and heads for the wine cellar. Harold turns back to the girls. "In Paris, it's said that if the Marquis De Sade had had a bottle of Chateau LaFite . . . his reputation might have even been a little . . . worse."

The girls lean in closer to encourage more of Harold's educated gossip, and Molly asks, "And how do you think that might have been possible?"

To which Holly adds, "Specifically."

Harold stretches forward, and in an animated way, whispers close to their faces.

The waiter returns, pours the wine, smiles, and leaves.

Then the members of the trio raise their glasses as Harold

62

makes a breathy toast. "May this be the most wildly passionate, unforgettably salacious . . . and shameful night of our lives."

Counterpointing the night's exciting plans for Harold and the girls, Jeffrey, back at the cabin, defines Janice's agenda for the rest of her stay. "You can have one shower and two cheese sandwiches."

CHAPTER FIFTEEN

Jeffrey picks a handful of darts off the mantle and positions himself in front of the dartboard that hangs on the wall next to the fireplace. Janice is in the rocking chair absorbing Jeffrey's 'house rules'. "Do not touch the TV. Do not touch the radio. Do not use the pink soap. Do not let water splash on the bathroom floor. Do not use the last of the toilet paper. And do not leave bread crumbs on the drainboard.

"If you make a mess anywhere in the house, clean it up, immediately. And do not even consider touching my toothbrush, or my harmonica."

Jeffrey throws his first dart. And though his accuracy is a little off, his form is exquisite. Then, after careful calculations for precise arm motion and graceful follow-through, his second dart nevertheless hits the wall several feet away from the dartboard.

Janice continues rocking, trying to ignore this revolting display of incompetence.

Finally, after three more throws, with only one actually hitting the dartboard, Janice is too disgusted to endure any more. She stands up and heads for the kitchen to make one of her two allotted cheese sandwiches, but then changes her mind, turns around, walks back to Jeffrey, and sticks out her hand. "May I?"

Reluctantly, Jeffrey places his last dart in Janice's hand.

Without hesitation, Janice aims and throws. The dart hits very close to the bullseye.

Janice walks out of the living room with Jeffrey's quarrelsome voice ready to follow her.

In the kitchen, as Janice gathers the ingredients for the cheese sandwich, Jeffrey calls out to her with important information, "That was not a bullseye, Janice."

Janice does not respond to his pettiness.

"Even if you only have a piece of bread, I'm counting it as a sandwich. Even if you only have one bite of cheese, I'm counting it as a sandwich."

Janice trims the edges off the bread and slices the cheese.

Jeffrey has additional information, "And I don't intend to be up all night listening to you bang around in the kitchen."

Still, she ignores him.

But, he still has advice quivering on his tongue, "So, you'd better make it a good sandwich, Janice, because it's the only one you're gonna get before your breakfast sandwich."

Janice puts the cheese back into the refrigerator, sweeps a few bread crumbs into the palm of her hand, drops them into the sink, picks up her sandwich, and leaves the kitchen.

She goes to the stack of firewood, picks off a log, pitches it into the fire, and sits down in the rocking chair.

Seething with resentment, Jeffrey crosses in front of her to place the darts on the mantle but stubs his toe in the process. Incoherently cursing with all his might, he hops wildly off into the kitchen on one foot. "Sonofabitchin' crapshit!!!"

Out of view, Jeffrey soon starts banging around and grumbling bits and pieces of passionate discontent. Then, following a sudden outburst of rapid unintelligible cursing, Jeffrey hops wildly back into view at the kitchen archway. He is livid. "How many times do I have to tell you?! If you make a mess, clean it up! It's called manners, Janice! It's called having consideration for others! It's called simple damn decency!"

Sandwich in hand, Janice gets out of the rocking chair, strolls into the kitchen past Jeffery, goes to the sink, turns on the faucet, swishes the bread crumbs down the drain, and shuts off the faucet. "Sorry, sometimes I'm just an inconsiderate bitch." Munching on her sandwich, she comments on her way out of the kitchen, "I could probably do better if I weren't so tired."

"Well, if you're tired, go to bed!"

Janice sinks wearily into the rocking chair. "I would if I knew where my bed was. Where is my bed?"

Jeffrey hobbles over to the fireplace. "You're rockin' in it." He sits on the stump and sets about tending the fireplace the way it's supposed to be tended. He pokes at the logs. "Geezuz, did you have to put that big log right on top of the little one, completely blocking any air from getting under it? Shit."

Janice ignores his stupid rant. "If I sleep in the rocking chair, where do you sleep?"

"I sleep in my bed."

"Does that sofa fold out into a bed?"

"Yes, Janice, it does. It folds out into my bed, where I sleep."

"I cannot sleep in a rocking chair."

"Tough. Go to a motel."

"I want to sleep in that bed."

Jeffrey is unshakably firm. "Not a chance, Janice."

"I will pay you an extra twenty-five dollars."

Jeffrey is steadfast. "There is not one single thing on this earth that could prevent me from sleeping in my own bed tonight. Is that sinking in? Are you starting to catch my drift?"

Janice is simply asking for a modicum of basic decency. "I just drove all the way from Florida, sixty-seven straight hours. Every bone in my body aches. I cannot sleep in a rocking chair. I have arthritis. Please, I beg you."

"God, what a whiney-cat."

Janice coughs. "I beg you."

"All right, all right! But the pillow belongs to me."

"You don't plan to sleep in there with me, do you?"

Jeffrey reacts: "Is this woman for real?"

Janice gets up and heads for the bathroom, picking up her carry-all bag enroute. "Okay, you can sleep there with me, but God help you if you try any funny business."

Janice enters the bathroom and closes the door behind her.

Jeffrey shrugs and mumbles to his dog, "God help her if she starts snoring."

CHAPTER SIXTEEN

Tilting drunkenly, Harold and the girls pass by the manager's front desk as they angle arm-in-arm for the elevator.

The manager speaks, "Good evening, Mr. Benson, ladies."

Harold responds, "Hey there."

The girls cleverly give the situation a reputable perception, "Daddy took us to dinner. It was sooo good."

Harold smiles in a parental way. "That's what daddies are for . . . taking care of their daughters."

The manager makes a mental note of this conversation.

Once they are on the elevator, Holly whispers, "Now, I think it's time for daddy's little girls to take care of daddy."

Harold smiles and pulls a key from his pocket. "Party in the penthouse!"

* * *

In the living room back at the cabin, the sound of the bathroom shower echoes as Jeffrey now prepares to write a country song. He opens an old trunk and takes out a pencil, a notebook, and his harmonica. He stokes up the flames, dims the lights, fills a champagne glass from a bottle of cheap wine, and lights a candle.

He then paces. Sips. Thinks. And finally sits on the stump, puts the harmonica to his lips, and plays a single note, signaling that he is now ready to put verse to music.

He mumbles to himself, "I see your face in the fireplace flames . . . and I want to say to you . . . you're the only one I'll ever love . . ."

He struggles to find the right word that rhymes with flames. "flames, flames . . . bames, games, stames, plames, trames, vames, wames, zames . . ."

Suddenly it comes to him, and he writes the word down. The shower sounds stop. Then, reading from his notebook, he now reviews the song with its newly completed verse. "I see your face in the fireplace flames . . . and I want to say to you . . . you're the only one I'll ever love . . . you're the prettiest . . . of all the dames."

The bathroom door opens wide enough for the most aggravating of all the dames to stick her towel-wrapped head through. "Do you have a pair of clean pajamas I can borrow?"

"Did you use the pink soap?"

"I did not. I have my own soap, thank you."

"Well, why didn't you bring your own pajamas?"

"I did. However, you're not the man I brought them to wear in front of."

"What are they, *Victoria's* latest *Secret* in crotchless sleepwear?"

"You are so crude. Would you mind just getting me a pair of pajamas?"

"I'm sorry, but I only have one pair of pajamas, and they're the ones I wear. So, I guess you're just outta luck."

"I can't sleep in my ski outfit. Do you have a jogging outfit I can borrow? One that's clean?"

"I don't wear jogging outfits, Janice. Usually, I just jog around in my old sweat pants with the big hole in the butt."

Janice is disgusted. "Well, what do you have . . . that's clean? A large T-shirt, maybe?"

With a curious smile, Jeffrey answers, "Yes, you can borrow the T-shirt my brother gave me. It's on the shelf in there next to the towels."

"Thank you." Janice closes the bathroom door.

Shortly, the bathroom door opens, and Janice walks out with the towel still wrapped around her head and a large white T-shirt draped to her knees. "I think your brother is a very sick individual."

Janice angles off to the kitchen, revealing the backside of

the T-shirt, where the face of a toothless old gold miner smiles through a big bushy mustache.

Above the face are the words, "FREE MOUSTACHE RIDES." And under the face: "NO FAT CHICKS ALLOWED."

Jeffrey has a moment of satisfaction before showing concern over Janice's kitchen privileges. "Why are you going into the kitchen, Janice?"

"I'm getting a glass of water, if you don't mind."

"Don't try to sneak any food while you're in there."

Janice walks out of the kitchen with a glass of water, goes to her side of the hearth, stands a log on end, sits on it, leans in close to the flames, and proceeds to towel-dry her hair.

Jeffrey doesn't like being intruded upon. "I'm not in your way, am I, Janice? It's okay if I continue to work here?"

"There's plenty of room here for both of us."

"Thank you for sharing my work area with me."

Jeffrey turns on the radio, and Hank Williams' voice sings softly in the background: "There's a tear in my beer, 'cause I'm crying for you, dear."

Janice is mildly curious about what Jeffrey does to make money. "What kind of work are you doing, anyway?"

"I happen to be writing a song."

Janice is concentrated on drying her hair, more or less indifferent to what Jeffrey has to say, but conversation, even one with a hillbilly, is a way of passing the time. She indicates to the radio. "Is that the kind of music you listen to, hillbilly music?"

"It's called country music, Janice. It's quite pleasant to the ear, and you can actually understand the lyrics. Probably not your kind of music."

"So, at night, you write country songs down here, and during the day, what do you do up there, in your office?"

"I write up there. Novels. And I might add, very important novels. Novels with staggering insights into the American culture. Novels that will lead Americans away from the abyss of frivolous behavior . . . and gratuitous cravings."

Janice's inner voice reacts, "Lucky us."

Janice's hair is still not dry, so she may as well continue 'killing time.' "Maybe I've read one. What are some of their titles?"

"There are no titles, Janice. The books are not yet published." Jeffrey takes a sip of wine. "And furthermore, I do not intend to title them until just moments before they go off to the printer. On a day which I fully expect to be in the very near future."

Janice fluffs her hair. "If they're so important, why haven't they been published?"

"Because the entire book publishing business is run by idiots and imbeciles. Even Louis L'Amour would have a hard time getting published nowadays."

"Then how do people like Cheri Huber, Melody Beattie, and Maya Angelou get published?"

"Never heard of them."

"They're all on the New York Times best-seller list."

73

"Sorry, not really interested in why butt-lifts and Botox are good financial investments."

"Last year, I wrote a little tongue-in-cheek article titled, *How to Spend Quality Time with Men Making Less Than a Hundred Thousand a Year*, and it got published. Forbes Magazine. December issue. They paid me forty-five hundred dollars for it."

"Ya know, Janice, you're really starting to get on my nerves."

Janice finishes drying her hair. "My, my . . . we're rather touchy about our career, aren't we?"

Janice stands up and moves to the sofa. She pulls at one end, but nothing happens. She moves to the other end and yanks hard, but still, nothing happens. She tries two or three more times, then looks over at Jeffrey. "Think you could give me a hand here?"

Without speaking, Jeffrey shoos her away, puts one hand behind his back, and, beaming with virtuosity, effortlessly uses his other hand to spring the sofa into a bed.

Janice gets into the bed. "I made one hundred and forty-seven thousand dollars last year. This year I should make at least twice that much. Good night."

Jeffrey looks at Janice, who is now under the covers with her back to him. He decides against giving her last remark any response. He turns off the radio and lowers himself back onto the tree stump, squarely facing the fire. His posture is reminiscent of a tired old cowboy sitting at a campfire at the end of the day.

74

He picks out a note on his harmonica, then sings softly, "I see your face in the fireplace flames."

Then comes the harmonica part.

Then it's more singing, "And I want to say to you."

Then a little more harmonica, followed by a little more singing, "You're the only one I'll ever love."

Again, comes the harmonica, followed by the song's most dramatic moment, "You're the prettiest of all the dames!"

At this point, the only unanswered question concerning his music is: of his voice, his lyrics, or his harmonica playing . . . which is the worst?

Jeffrey is nearly 'spent,' but still seated on the stump, hunched over, silhouetted by the fire's glow, gathering his strength for the final verse.

Janice is in bed with her hands clamped over her ears, just hoping to survive this whole scene without bursting into gut-wrenching laughter.

Jeffrey now slides into the scintillating final verse, "But then I saw you cheatin' on me in Bubba's pickup truck,

"So, I hopped a freight train to Galveston,

"And I started drinking red red wine,

"For my blue blue heart,

"And now I'm here in prison,

"And even though they're gonna hang me in the morning,

"Just tell my momma that it's okay,

"Because I'll be goin' to the land of broken hearts,

75

Here comes the clever part, "Where I'll be king . . . every day."

Jeffrey now blows a lengthy freight-train-dog-whistle-wailing harmonica, as Janice is under the covers, silently, but spasmodically, writhing in contortions of stifled hysteria.

CHAPTER SEVENTEEN

The penthouse accommodations are ultra-lavish, with a breathtaking view of Lake Tahoe. On a bear-skin rug in front of a fake-log, push-button fireplace, two young girls wearing scant negligees and Santa Claus hats frolic with a man twice their age.

Harold drums a beat on Holly's butt as though it were a set of bongos, while Molly–astride Harold's shoulders–slaps his head like a congo drum, as the drunken trio attempts to harmonize their personal recollections of the lyrics to the Christmas music playing on the radio.

"Twelves drummers drumming . . . eleven pipers piping . . . ten lords a-leaping . . . nine ladies dancing . . . eight maids a-milking . . . seven swans a-swimming . . . six geese a-laying . . .

"Five golden rings . . .

"Four calling birds, three French hens, two turtle doves . . .

A staccato of drumbeats now precede Harold's big solo finish ". . . and some naked babes to wrap around me!"

CHAPTER EIGHTEEN

As dawn breaks over the mountaintops, Jeffrey pops out of bed, brushes his teeth, makes coffee, and bounds up the stairs to disappear into his office.

Janice wakes up annoyed and goes into the bathroom. Minutes later, clothed but rumpled, she leaves the bathroom, enters the kitchen, and makes a cup of instant coffee. She then takes the folded Kleenex from her shirt pocket, unwraps her two cigarettes, breaks one in half, re-wraps the remaining one and a half, and tucks them carefully back into her pocket. She then lights up, takes her first sip of morning coffee, then takes her first, long, glorious, inhalation of morning nicotine.

Jeffrey is suddenly heard pounding down the stairs. He goes directly to the bookcase to once again search around. Finding nothing, he then moves the barstool to the window, climbs it, reaches up for the vase, and checks for contents. But it's still empty. He then returns the barstool back to its proper place and dashes back up to his office.

Janice rolls her eyes and is about to 'squirrel away' the now quarter-inch cigarette butt, when she has a sudden change of mind. She leaves the kitchen, moves the barstool back in front of the window, climbs it, stretches up onto her tiptoes, drops the tiny cigarette butt into the vase, and returns the barstool to its usual place.

Janice's spirits are immediately elevated by the thrill of her mischief, and she hums as she proceeds to make the bed. However, it then occurs to her that she is not required to make the bed, and so she messes it back into disarray.

She checks her wristwatch, picks up her cat, sits in the rocking chair, pulls a *Cosmopolitan* magazine from her purse, and notices the title of the featured article: "Does Your Man Have a Roving Eye . . . and Could Breast Implants Be an Answer?"

Janice rolls her eyes in disgust and opens the magazine to an article titled: *"Ten Ways to Build Financial Security."*

She then relaxes into reading the article, rocking, stroking her cat, and waiting for the plow to arrive.

* * *

Time passes. Janice looks at her wristwatch, stands up, stretches, and goes into the kitchen. She makes another cup of coffee, unwraps her cigarettes, and is soon engaged in a half-cigarette, late-morning smoke, when once again Jeffrey is heard bounding down the stairs.

Janice watches from the kitchen as he hurries over to the bookcase.

Searching quickly but finding nothing, he immediately gets the barstool into position in front of the window, climbs it, reaches into the vase, and, lo and behold, finds a tiny cigarette butt. He pockets it, returns the vase to the valance, returns the barstool to its place, and returns to his office.

Janice shrugs to herself. 'Whatever.'

On her way back to the rocking chair, Janice becomes interested in the expensive-looking telescope aimed out the window towards the mountaintop. Moving it around, Janice focuses on different things: trees, sky, more trees, more sky, then, interestingly enough, Janice can bring Sky Tavern into focus.

And as luck would have it, there on the private penthouse deck, Harold, Molly, and Holly–wearing only sopping wet Santa hats–sit in a bubbling spa, looking spacey-eyed and worn out, with their mouths dropped open and their shoulders hunched forward.

This view is suddenly disrupted when the telescope hits the floor as Janice, gasping for breath, bolts for the door, leaving it ajar as she runs off crying hysterically.

CHAPTER NINETEEN

It's lunchtime. Jeffrey comes out of the loft and heads for the kitchen. Noticing the front door is open, he angles off to close it, mumbling as he goes, speaking for Janice, "Thank you again Jeffrey, appreciate all your help, just thought I'd leave the damn door open for ya."

He then notices the unmade bed. "And your damn bed all messed up."

He then notices the telescope on the floor. "Plus, I decided to knock over your damn telescope."

But just before pulling the door closed, Jeffrey's ears are alerted to some faint sound coming from outdoors. He stretches his neck out the door and aims his ears. Then he hears it again, more distinctly. It's Janice yelling from below the edge of the cliff just beyond the sign reading: DANGER. CLIFF AREA. KEEP OUT.

Jeffrey grabs the coiled rope off the nearby wall peg, dashes up the stairs, and hits the red button. Outside, his truck engine revs up, and he yanks on the pulley rope. The hayloft door swings open, and Jeffrey races through it, somersaulting downwards to his idling truck.

He misses.

But he quickly kicks his way up out of the surrounding snowbank, jumps into his truck, peels a doughnut, and is off to the rescue. Plowing through the heavy snow, the truck skids up dangerously close to the edge of the cliff. Rope in hand, Jeffrey jumps out of the truck and can immediately see Janice hanging precariously from a dead tree branch wedged into a crevice on the side of the cliff wall!

Jeffrey twirls the rope over his head and lets it fly. It smacks into Janice's face, knocking her loose and sending her plummeting towards the rocky river raging through the deep gorge below. Miraculously, she crashes into the only living tree protruding from the cliff's wall. She's momentarily spared until the branches that have caught her begin cracking and snapping under the pressure of her weight!

Yelling and grasping at everything sliding past her, Janice somehow manages to grab hold of the last substantial branch, leaving her dangling hopelessly above her certain doom!

Jeffrey quickly reels in the rope, twirls it, and lets it fly! The lasso hits on top of Janice's head and falls down around her neck. Her face registers concern over the possible consequences regarding this latest development.

The rope tightens securely around her windpipe as Jeffrey yells out his emergency instructions! "Don't panic! I'll have you out of there before you can say 'Jack Frost!'"

Jeffrey quickly ties the rope around his front bumper, jumps into his truck, slams it into reverse . . . and shortly thereafter, Janice's limp body rises up over the edge of the cliff where Jeffrey can then drag her safely away from the precipice.

"Geezuz, Janice! You're not supposed to have that around your neck! You're supposed to have it around your waist!"

He then fumbles his way through a somewhat lengthy extrication of the noose. "You could have been killed! You're lucky you didn't break your neck! I better get you back to the cabin, pronto!"

CHAPTER TWENTY

Time has passed, the fireplace burns brightly, and Janice, in bed, buried under the covers, has been sleeping like a baby. She now starts to revive, and Jeffrey's face is the first thing that comes slowly into her focus. He speaks, "Thank God you're okay. You've been in a coma for over two hours, but you're gonna be all right."

He inspects her eyes. "You'll be a little dizzy for a while, and it will be hard for you to remember things, but eventually, everything will come back to you. To start with, your name is Janice Jones."

With her eyes barely open, Janice speaks in a voice too weak and slurred for Jeffrey to understand, "Yiyoyuyiyam yuyidya."

Jeffrey leans an ear closer to Janice's mouth. "I'm sorry, I can't quite understand what you're saying."

Janice raises her voice slightly. "I said, 'I know who I am, you idiot.'"

Jeffrey is appalled. "Well, excuse me! Excuse me for saving your life after I pulled your car out of the snowbank and provided you with food and shelter while you were wrecking my whole entire life!"

Unnoticed by either Jeffrey or Janice, a snowblower can be seen through the front window, cutting a path up to the cabin.

Gathering her strength, Janice sits up. "What life?! You call this a life?!"

"At least I don't have a tattoo on my tits!"

"And just exactly how do you know that I have a very small, tastefully done rose tattoo on one of my breasts!"

"Because, when I was getting you out of your wet clothes so that you wouldn't catch pneumonia and die, I saw your tits, Janice! Both of them!"

"Did you fondle me too, you degenerate hillbilly!"

"If I had fondled you, Janice, I wouldn't be here right now! I'd be down at the doctor's office getting my eyes examined!"

"You are the most despicable, repulsive, reprehensible slimeball I have ever known!"

At this point, the front door opens, and Harold Benson, blocked from seeing Jeffrey and Janice by the high stack of firewood, pokes his head inside. "Hello?"

Harold's voice catches Janice by surprise, but she instantly recovers and throws her arms around Jeffrey's neck. "Take me!"

Jeffrey reacts: "Huh?"

"Take me!"

"Take you?"

"Take me like a drunken sailor!" Janice now grabs Jeffrey's hands and yanks them to her breasts.

Jeffrey, pulled face forward into her lap with his arms stretched upward, is pinned awkwardly into this position by her grasp of his hands against her breasts.

Harold moves towards Janice's voice but is then stopped in his tracks by what he sees. "Janice!"

Janice turns to Harold. "Oh no! I'm caught! Cheating on you!"

Harold is outraged. "Well, I'm certainly glad I saw this side of you before we got married!"

Harold stomps out, slamming the door behind him.

Janice flinches from the loud slam, then turns back to Jeffrey and slaps him in the face. "You pervert!"

Janice now breaks into tears, pulls the covers over her head, and immediately begins sobbing uncontrollably. Jeffrey is overcome with guilt and, anxious to make amends, directs his voice at the lump under the covers. "Janice, I'm sorry about what just happened. I think my hands just made an innocent accident. Can I get you something? Soup or something? I could make you some eggs."

Janice's voice is difficult to understand through the sobbing. "Kleenex."

But Jeffrey tries. "Clean eggs? You want me to wash some eggs?"

Janice pronounces the word more clearly, "Kleeeenex."

"Kleenex. Oh. Okay. I thought you said clean eggs." Jeffrey now decides to add a little ill-advised humor to the moment. "I was wondering what kind of soap to use, should I use hand soap, or dish soap, or . . . okay, sorry. I'll be right back, Janice. I'm going to get Kleenex. I'll be back in . . . eight seconds."

Jeffrey hurries off to the bathroom, then quickly returns with a roll of toilet paper and hands it under the covers. "I'm out of Kleenex, but I have toilet paper. It's just as good.

"It's actually better. It's stronger. This is the two-ply kind. It's more expensive, but in the long run, it's cheaper because you don't have to fold it so many times. Usually, I just fold it over once, then use it, then fold it over again, and–"

Janice interrupts Jeffrey's comments by blowing her nose, very loudly.

Jeffrey wants desperately to help. He sits gently on the bed and strokes the lump. "I'm not exactly sure why you're crying. I think I know but, I'm not quite totally positive. If I knew exactly, then I could talk to you about it, and I think it would be very helpful."

But the sobbing continues, deeper and sadder.

Jeffrey renews his efforts. "Let me take a shot at it. I'll tell you what I think just happened, and you correct me if I start to get a little off track. Okay?

"Is this what happened? You started getting turned on when I was talking about your breasts, and you suddenly wanted me so badly that you lost all your morals, and then your fiancé saw us, and you immediately realized that there wouldn't be any wedding, and that you'd never see Harold again.

"Was that it? Was that what happened?"

Through the gulping, desperate, painful sobbing, Janice manages to answer, "No."

Jeffrey is more determined than ever to be helpful. "Okay. Let me try again. When I was talking about your breasts, you got upset and decided to go home, and so when you said 'take me,' what you meant was 'take you home.' Was that it?"

With a reinvigorated durability, the sobbing grows more heartbreaking until Janice can barely manage to utter more than a single word, "No."

Jeffrey is devastated, but soldiers on. "Was it because I saw your breasts, and they looked kind of small and–"

A loud, crestfallen moan suddenly erupts from under the covers when the size of Janice's breasts is mentioned, causing Jeffrey to make one, almost final, effort to understand the cause of all this sadness. "Did you want me to touch your breasts so that I would know they were bigger than they looked when you were lying on your back . . . in case I was ever going to describe you in a novel?"

But that question only ignites deeper, louder, and more heartbreaking moaning, leaving Jeffrey with his last and final option. "Was it because your breasts itched?"

Janice turns over onto her back and pulls the covers tighter. "I saw Harold, through the telescope, cheating on me . . . with some tramp. Two tramps. It was so humiliating, he was being," she can hardly say the word, "kinky!"

"Oh."

The sobbing recedes; Janice hasn't eaten breakfast or lunch, so she is starving. "Would you make me a sandwich?"

Jeffrey is very eager to help in any way he can. "Absolutely. What kind of sandwich do you want?"

"Egg salad."

Jeffrey springs into action. "Is that hard-boiled eggs chopped up with mayonnaise in it?"

"Yes."

Jeffrey un-springs. "I'm out of mayonnaise."

"It doesn't matter. Nothing matters."

"No! That's not true! It does matter! Everything matters! That's what life is all about. If you're out of mayonnaise, go for it anyway!"

Janice can barely muster even a feeble attempt at understanding. "What does that even mean?"

"I'll tell you what it means! It means that you shouldn't cry over spilt milk! That you've got to pick yourself up, dust yourself off, and get back in the race!"

Janice really would like something to eat. "Instead of an egg salad sandwich, could you make me a tuna fish sandwich on toast?"

Jeffrey claps his hands together in a very inspiring way. "Yes! I can! I will! Immediately!" He heads sprightly towards the kitchen, but again makes a sudden U-turn and returns to the bed. "I'm out of mayonnaise."

"It doesn't matter."

"Janice, please! When the going gets tough, the tough get going! Tomorrow is another day!"

"Could I have it without the mayonnaise?"

"Tuna on toast hold the mayo. Okay. You want onions?"

"Lots."

"Okay, Janice, you got it!"

Jeffrey hurries into the kitchen and gets busy making Janice a sandwich while at the same time relating to her a very inspirational personal experience. "Janice, let me tell you a personal story that you might find inspiring. It's about a guy who writes a book and sends it off to a publisher."

Jeffrey opens a can of tuna fish as he's speaking. "And every morning, he goes to his mailbox hoping to find a letter from the publisher informing him that they would like to publish his book."

Jeffrey chops up a large onion, causing his eyes to tear up. "And day after day, the letter does not arrive. And days pass into weeks, and weeks into months, until finally one morning there is a letter in the mailbox from the publisher, and he rips it open, and it reads as follows . . ."

Janice pokes her head out from under the covers and sits up, making it easier for her to listen.

"Dear writer, we're sorry, but we will not be publishing your book."

Onion tears stream down Jeffrey's face as he enters the living room to deliver Janice's sandwich and finish the inspirational story. "Although we do not believe your book to be totally without merit, we find it difficult to understand why you chose to make your central character such a moron."

Janice tries to make Jeffrey feel better. "Maybe if you rewrote it and made your central character a little smarter, maybe then the publishers would–"

"The book is an autobiography, Janice."

"Oh. I'm sorry."

"That's okay. They're just idiots and imbeciles. The point is, you've got to keep trying." Jeffrey sits on the bed while Janice eats her sandwich. "How do you feel now, better?"

"Yes."

"Good. Let's just keep talking. It's good for you. It's therapeutic."

"Okay."

Jeffrey takes a deep breath. "What would you like to talk about?"

Janice settles into a more comfortable position. "I don't know. Anything. Sex?"

"Sex? Really?"

"Well, it's not like something we never think about, is it?"

"No."

"Well then?"

Jeffrey chuckles nervously. "It's just kind of weird to talk to a girl about sex."

"You think it's more natural to talk to a boy about it?"

"No. It's just that girls are so, you know."

"No, I don't know. What do you mean 'they're so,' what?"

"You know . . ."

"Shy about the subject?"

"Yeah. They never like to, you know . . ."

"Talk openly about it?"

"Yeah."

"You know what I think it is? I think it's just that girls place a higher value on physical intimacy. With girls, it's not just some testosterone-driven gymnastic-gratification like it is for boys."

Jeffrey is offended. "What?"

"That's right. Boys are like animals. Their brains are all in their crotch."

"That, is pure, baloney."

"No, it's not. Boys see a naked . . . anything, a shoulder, a belly button, a breast, and suddenly they've gotta . . . 'do it.'"

"They don't even have to see a breast. Somebody can just tell them there's a naked breast in the area, and they'll go nuts figuring out how to get their filthy little hands on it."

Jeffrey feels personally insulted. "That is so ridiculous."

Janice enjoys being the provocateur. "You mean you can see a naked breast and not instantly turn into a shifty-eyed, conniving, little weasel?"

"What do you think I am, some kind of rabid dog in heat!?"

Janice smiles. "I think if I showed you any of my private areas, you would lose complete control of yourself and immediately start scheming a way to 'get me.'"

"I most certainly would not."

Janice challenges him, "I bet you would."

Jeffery accepts this absurd provocation. "I'll bet you twenty bucks."

"Okay, it's a bet."

Jeffrey now reacts with great self-control to Janice's increasingly erotic attempts to 'turn him on.' And even if Janice hadn't moved into a poorly lit area, it would be easy enough to imagine, more or less, what she is doing based on their dialogue.

She starts with a question, "Okay. How's that?"

Jeffrey scoffs. "Nothing. I don't feel a thing. It just looks like a regular old breast to me."

"How about when I do this?"

"Nope. Nothing."

"How about this?"

Jefferey coughs. "Nope."

"How about when I do this?"

A slight hesitancy is noticed in Jeffrey's voice. "No."

94

Janice's voice now sounds a bit strained. "How about this?"

There is a short delay before his response. "No."

"Are you sure?"

Jeffrey answers unconvincingly, "Yes."

"Are you sure you're being absolutely honest with me?"

Beads of sweat slide down Jeffrey's forehead. "Yes. I admit I do find it marginally interesting . . . in a technical sense."

Still straining, Janice responds, "Technical sense?"

"Yes. I used to be quite a good gymnast myself. And I know how technically difficult it is to keep your balance when you're standing on your head and moving your legs around like that."

Janice concedes. "Okay, you win. I'm amazed at your self-control. I owe you twenty bucks."

Janice has, presumably, just rolled out of a headstand and now assumes a modest sitting position back on the bed. "I've never done anything like that before."

Jeffrey is humble in victory. "Maybe now you won't be so quick to judge the motives of your fellow human beings."

Jeffrey stands up from the bed to go to the kitchen, bending and stooping in ways that might be recognized as the manly art of leaving a room without revealing an erection. "May I get you another sandwich or a wass of glotter?"

Janice looks at him. "A wass of glotter?"

Jeffery can also be deceitful, dishonest, and duplicitous in victory. "I didn't say wass of glotter."

"What did you say?"

"I said glass of water."

Janice nods. "Oh. Water. Yes please."

As he hunches off to the kitchen, Jeffrey attempts a flimsy explanation as to why he is walking so oddly. "I think I twisted my vertebrates. Yesterday. Before you got here. While I was carrying a boulder. On my shoulder. It was huge."

In the kitchen, Jeffrey quickly moves to an area out of Janice's line of sight and proceeds to shift and readjust the bulge of his erection.

Janice has gotten up and now sits, wrapped in her blanket, on the tree stump, gazing into the fire.

Jeffrey, projecting an aloof demeanor, returns to the living room and speaks as he hands Janice her glass of water. "Do you like kids, Janice?"

"I used to want a whole bunch."

"What happened to that dream?"

"Finished college. Started a career. Loved the job. Worked hard. Became successful. Met Harold."

Jeffrey sits down on the bed facing Janice's backside. She speaks into the fire, and he speaks to the back of her head with an off-handed remark, "I suppose it would be okay if you wanted to read some of my writing."

Janice responds absently, "No reason not to."

Jeffery casually suggests, "Maybe I ought to go up to my office and get a page from my new novel?"

Janice nods, "Okay."

Jeffrey heads lackadaisically up the stairs, speaking to Janice without looking at her. "Should I bring down a page that I wrote last week, or something I wrote on the day we met?"

"Maybe something you wrote on the day we met."

"All right then, that's what I'll do."

Jeffrey enters his office and the curtains close behind him. He immediately moves about with a swift, very focused sense of purpose: to the shaving cabinet for a swipe of cologne, onto the floor for a pushup, into his desk for the page from his novel, back to the cabinet for another swipe of cologne, and then . . . mirror-check.

Mirror-check means teeth-check, nose-hair check, and lastly, before his last stop in the bathroom, he makes a 'special face' . . . whereby he pulls a comb back through his hair as he curls a lip, just like Elvis.

Janice gets up from the stump and meanders across the room to a small framed picture of Jeffrey at four years of age, laughing and running across a lawn, being chased by a puppy. She studies it.

She then sets the picture down and crosses to the telescope, debating whether to look through it. She puts her hand on it, but hesitates, frozen by indecision. Then she pushes the telescope slowly away and returns to sit on the stump and gaze back into the fire.

As Jeffrey comes matter-of-factly through the loft curtains and heads down the stairs, it is immediately noticed that he no longer has a beard. He steps into the living room but stops short of Janice.

She turns around from the fire expecting a bearded man to put a page from his novel into her hand. But instead, the clean-shaven man standing in front of her curls a lip and pulls a comb back through his hair.

Janice doesn't quite understand what is going on, but asks about it as she reaches out for the page. "What's the matter?"

"What do you mean?"

"Your face just went like this," she answers, imitating special-face.

"It did?"

"Yes."

Jeffrey thinks fast. "Oh, I know what must have happened. My tongue must have gone over to the side of my mouth to get a seed that was stuck in my teeth. It was a boysenberry seed that got in there when I was reading the Bible the day before you got here. It was stuck in there. Yeah. And my tongue was trying to get it out. And that's why my face just got all scrunched around."

"Your beard is gone."

"I shaved it off."

"You look so much more . . . courteous."

"Thank you."

Jeffrey takes the lit candle off the mantle and hands it to Janice. She places the page from his novel onto her knees, and is now ready to read by candlelight.

"Uno momento." Jeffrey takes two glasses and a bottle of wine out of a nearby trunk, hands a glass to Janice, fills it, fills the other, and offers a toast. "Here's to kids with dirty faces and the puppies that chase them . . . to crayon drawings on refrigerator doors . . . to evenings without television . . . to pancakes and cartoons on Saturday mornings . . . to smarty-pants women with pony-tails, wearing blue jeans and earrings . . . and here's to having someone to hold onto when life is knocking you sideways."

Their eyes lock onto each other for just a moment before they tap glasses.

Then Jeffrey speaks, "But first, before you start reading . . ."

Jeffrey retrieves a pillow from the trunk. Then, after first sliding the stump awkwardly–with Janice still sitting on it–he manages to push it across the wax line and into 'his territory' to be closer to the warm fire.

He then plugs an electrical cord into a wall socket, and the Christmas tree is finally brought to life. "Okay. Now you can read. And I won't bother you again. I'll just wait until you're done before I say anything."

Janice, with the wine in one hand and a candle in the other, now reads.

Jeffrey paces around, watching her intensely.

Janice soon reacts to something on the page. Jeffery moves closer and bends over her shoulder to see what it is. But his encroachment causes her to lose concentration, and he quickly backs away to continue pacing.

Eventually, Janice turns to Jeffrey. "I've got to be honest with you, I'm having a little trouble with the first sentence."

"First sentence? You've been reading all this time, and you're still on the first sentence?"

"Once I get past that first sentence . . ."

Jeffrey moves closer to have a look at that first sentence.

"What's the problem? How can you be having trouble with that?"

"Well, I guess it's the believability factor that I'm having trouble with."

"Why? It's the story of how America's whole value system is being corrupted by celebrities." Jeffrey continues like a man on a mission. "Like the 'self-help' television gurus who 'book' the most depressed people they can find, encourage them to divulge, in detail, the unbearable heart-breaking experience which ruined their life . . . then nod in a most sympathetic way and offer some cheesy solution to their problems.

"And like those money-grubbing celebrity preachers that swarm the Sunday television channels hustling their cut-rate tickets to heaven.

"And the celebrity spokesperson who, for a million-dollar paycheck, will speak sincerely about the nutritional value of porcupine poop.

"And the twenty-five-year-old celebrity rock stars who spend more on their weekly drugs than the average guy makes in a year . . . then sing about how unfair life is.

"And the celebrity athletes, whining because some player who evidently consumes more steroids than they do . . . makes twenty million a year while they're only making eighteen.

"And the political celebrities, with their deeply felt ethical values . . . dictated entirely by lobbyists, poll numbers, and campaign contributions.

"And that three-legged turkey of self-importance, the most obnoxious celebrities of all . . . the reality stars whose greatest talent is going to the gym, the Botox doctor, and the tanning salon . . . in preparation for taking their shirt off and ranting at least ten obscenities from their twenty-word vocabularies."

With Janice now giving him her full attention, Jeffrey is encouraged to continue, "We're letting the celebrities determine what our personal values should be. We're not sitting around the campfire figuring things out for ourselves anymore. We're just buying the 'labels' and following the 'crowd.'

"And the celebrities are even more nuts than we are because they actually believe that they deserve to be followed around.

"And that's what my novel is all about: the evilness of celebrities. A fictionalized account of what these people are 'really' like."

Janice considers what has just been explained to her. "You seem a little worked up over all this."

"Read that first sentence out loud, and I think you'll see what I'm getting at."

Janice reads: "Slowly, cocking her 357 as she pulls away

from her naked sex slave, Judge Judy snarls . . . 'Die you scum-sucking swine of a devil whore pig.'"

Janice looks up from the page.

Jeffrey is satisfied. "Starting to make a little more sense now?"

Janice is ready to change the subject. "I should probably start at the beginning of the book."

"Yeah, that's probably the best way to do it."

Janice stands up, sets the page and the candle onto the mantle, then sits on the bed and pulls the covers up over her knees.

Jeffrey sits on the bed across from her.

She asks, "Are you a smoker?"

"No, I'm a non-smoker! I quit one year ago. Cold turkey.

"Okay, yes, I recently did have one tiny little partial ciga-rette, but I didn't inhale. So, legally, I'm just the same as a non-smoker."

He leans toward Janice's face. "Here, smell my breath."

Janice leans away. "I don't need to smell your breath."

Jeffrey leans closer. "Smell. I'm not lying."

Janice ducks her face away, but Jeffrey pursues, "Please, Janice."

Janice ducks again. Jeffrey extends himself even more. "Please, just one little sniff."

Jeffrey's mouth is attacking Janice's nose. "Just one little sniff, is that asking too much?"

Janice finally puts an end to it. "Jeffrey! For God's sake! Get a grip!"

At this point, they are about to cross a barrier and do the most intimate thing that two people can do: be 'playful' with each other.

Jeffrey smiles and looks Janice squarely in the eyes. "No thanks."

At which point, he reaches over and takes Janice's hand, and clamps his teeth onto her index finger.

She reacts, "Now what in the hell are you doing?"

Jeffrey smiles without opening his mouth.

Janice gives him a look of disgust and indicates to her finger. "You expect to be on there long?"

Jeffrey nods yes, sending a ripple up Janice's arm.

"How long?"

Jeffrey shrugs his shoulders.

"Oh, I see. We're playing a little power game here." Janice arranges herself into a more comfortable position. "Okay, no problem, I'll play this little game with you. I can outlast you any day of the week."

The game continues. Before long, Janice leans her face out to the end of her arm, where she speaks to Jeffrey's face, "Your jaw getting a little tired?"

Jeffrey shakes his head, wagging Janice's arm in the process.

Janice sits back into an even more comfortable position. "I can easily outlast you. All I have to do is sit here. You're the one who has to do all the work. You're the one who's going to get a sore jaw. I can sit like this all night."

Janice crosses her legs and rests her chin in the palm of her free hand. She looks quite comfortable, aside from her outstretched arm leading into Jeffrey's face.

A few moments pass before she reaches over, pinches Jeffrey's nostrils shut, and twists his nose. He cries out in pain, causing his mouth to release Janice's finger.

Janice justifies her tactic: "But I don't want to sit like that all night."

Jeffrey laughs and sits back. "You didn't have to twist so hard."

Janice replies, "Let that be a lesson to you."

Now they both stretch around to get comfortable.

Jeffrey broaches a different subject, "So, what happens next, Janice?"

Janice fluffs the pillow. "What happens next?

Jeffrey nods. "Yeah, after tonight."

"Well, in the morning, the sun is gonna come up, and I'm gonna leave."

"Where are you going?"

"Back to my life."

"The one with Harold in it?"

"Yes."

"Why?"

Janice thinks before answering, "Have you ever been poor, Jeffrey? Really poor?"

"No."

Janice takes a deep breath and tells him her story. "I was born into a wonderful family . . . that was dirt poor. We were what people called hillbillies. My daddy had decided early on that he wasn't going to spend his life trying to make lots of money. And that suited my momma just fine.

"It was a simple way of living. Daddy and my brothers cut the firewood, built the fires, kept the truck running, fixed the plumbing, patched the roof, fed the hounds . . . all that kind of stuff.

"And Momma and I did the cooking and cleaning, and sewed the patches on their britches . . . all that kind of stuff.

"They told us kids to always be proud of our independence. And I always was. Until my senior prom.

"I didn't go because I didn't have a dress pretty enough to wear.

"It hurt, and I vowed to never again miss another dance because I didn't have a dress pretty enough to wear."

"What about Harold?"

Janice sighs. "We'll talk. We'll patch things up. Last August, we opened our own advertising agency. On paper, in just this first year, we can project a guaranteed net income of almost four hundred thousand dollars."

Jeffrey considers what she has just said and repeats her resolution, "So, you'll be leaving in the morning."

Janice smiles. "You sound like you might miss me."

Jeffrey laughs. "Like I don't have enough problems just getting this country back on track? I need a few more? Like somebody twisting my nose? Or leaving crumbs in the sink?"

Their faces are close together. They look into each other's eyes. It appears that they are about to kiss, but they hesitate, and the moment passes as Janice turns away and wraps herself a little tighter into the covers. "I hope you have a wonderful life, Jeffrey."

Trapped by his own words, Jeffrey is left with little to say. "I hope you have a wonderful life too." Jeffrey reaches down and eases the electrical cord out of the wall socket, cutting the life out of the Christmas tree. He then wraps his half of the covers over his shoulders and lays down, leaving a wide space between his back and hers.

Two sad, mixed-up people are about to spend their last night together, alone. "Happy New Year, Jeffrey."

"Happy New Year, Janice."

CHAPTER TWENTY-ONE

It is freezing cold as the sun breaks over the mountains. A driver stands alongside an open limousine door waiting for Janice. "Sky Tavern" is lettered across its door.

Jeffrey is on the front porch.

Inside, Janice takes one last look around as if to etch an everlasting picture into her memory.

Before leaving, she has one last thing to do: she positions the barstool, takes the carefully folded Kleenex from her shirt pocket, unfolds it, looks at her 'treasure,' climbs onto the barstool, raises up onto her tiptoes, and drops her last cigarette into the vase. Janice then walks out of the cabin and closes the door behind her. And with her cat in her arms, she now faces Jeffrey. She is ready to leave. "Goodbye, Jeffrey. I will never forget you."

Jeffrey pauses, then speaks in a whisper, "I hope you have children someday."

Janice hurries off the porch and into the limo. The driver shuts the door, and they leave. She does not look back.

CHAPTER TWENTY-TWO

In the dining room at the lodge, Harold and Janice sit at a table across from each other. The waiter refills their wine glasses. Apparently, they have talked, patched things up, and are back about their business of vacationing. Harold appears to be satisfied with the arrangement and is attentive to Janice. She appears passively willing to accept his efforts.

* * *

Back at the cabin, Jeffrey sits on the stump in front of the fireplace and stares into the fire, which is now nothing more than glowing embers. Evidently, he has been sitting this way, without tending the fire, for a long period of time.

* * *

The following day, Janice and Harold ride a chair lift skyward. Seen from a distance, Harold talks, while Janice listens, absently.

* * *

Jeffrey sits in his office, staring vacantly into space and doodling onto a page already overflowing with doodles.

* * *

Later that day, in the lodge bar, at the hub of an after-ski crowd, Harold laughs and enjoys himself while Janice is conspicuously uninvolved in the social interactions.

* * *

In the kitchen, Jeffrey makes his power-shake. His movements in filling the blender are now simply done in rote. When he unenthusiastically pitches a banana across the room, he's unconcerned that it misses the blender and lands on the floor; he merely steps over it.

* * *

Harold and Janice are in bed. Moonlight streams through the sliding glass doors leading to the balcony. Their voices are heard coming from the shadows.

Harold attempts to sound reasonable, "I don't see why we can't just . . . you know.

"I said I was sorry.

"Eventually, we're gonna start doing it again anyway, so . . .

"I mean . . . why waste a good vacation."

Janice asks, "Harold, how much do you love me?"

Harold pauses for effect, then answers, "A lot."

"How much is a lot?"

It has been a long day, and they are both tired, but Harold is willing to 'go the extra mile.' "Very much. Very, very much. You are more precious to me . . . than all the stars in the sky."

But his poetic proclivities soon ebb into soft snoring.

Janice gets out of bed and drapes on a robe while moving towards the balcony. She steps into the cold night air under a black sky with bright stars and a full moon pouring through the treetops. Pulling her robe tighter, she leans against the balcony rail and eases into some personal dream.

* * *

Jeffrey, nursing his power-shake, sits zombie-like in front of the television set where old-time cowboys are gunfighting, barroom brawling, and jumping on horses to high-tail it. Eventually, with the power-shake still in hand, he turns the television off, walks into the bathroom, and stands in front of the mirror to evaluate himself.

Expressionless, he then walks out of the bathroom and into the kitchen, opens the refrigerator, and looks at the food. Moments pass, he closes the refrigerator, and leaves the kitchen. He goes to the fireplace mantle, picks up his harmonica, looks at it, and lobs it softly into the fireplace. He then stares at it half-buried in the ashes, bends down and picks it up, stares at it again, and, still expressionless, lobs it back into the ashes.

He crosses the room and stands in front of the window, looking up the mountain at the haze of soft light coming from Sky Tavern. Eventually, without changing the blankness of his expression, he looks into the telescope. After several small adjustments, he brings the bright full moon into view . . . with Janice's face profiled in the center of it. He watches her return to her room.

Tension grows in his demeanor until . . . Jeffrey slams the blender into the fireplace and charges up the stairs. He pounds his fist onto the red button, and as his truck is heard starting up, he yanks on the pulley rope. The hayloft door swings open, and Jeffrey somersaults coat-less into the moonlight.

He lands on the truck's roof, backflips onto the ground, jumps into the driver's seat, spins a doughnut, and roars off. Within seconds, the truck runs out of gas and sputters to a stop.

Jeffrey slams his fist against the dashboard, jumps out of the truck, and races off. He reaches the highway and heads uphill at a furious pace until a huge, yellow snowplow, thundering wildly down the highway, throws off a six-foot wave of heavy snow. It knocks Jeffrey backward into an embankment, burying him in cold, wet, dirty slush.

Clawing his way back to his feet, Jeffrey advances. Panting like a dog and sweating like a pig, Jeffrey fights his way through the frigid night, headed for his woman. It's a long, cold, painful effort that eventually leaves him shivering and exhausted as he finally staggers through the Sky Tavern gates.

Gasping for breath, he struggles through the courtyard of the chalet. Exhaling clouds of frozen vapor, Jeffrey yells up to the empty balconies, "Janice! Janice! Where are you!"

Confused, frightened people peek cautiously out between their closed curtains.

Hearing all the commotion, Harold and Janice sit up in bed.

Harold reacts, "What the hell?"

Janice reacts, "Could it be a terrorist?"

Harold gets out of bed, throws on a robe, and as he moves through the darkness, bangs into something. He reacts, "Sonofabitch!"

Janice reacts to Harold's reaction. "Are you shot?!"

"No!"

"Do you need a tourniquet?"

"I just broke my friggin' nose!"

Now, louder and more urgent, Jeffrey calls again, "Janice! Janice!"

Harold jerks the balcony's glass door open and storms out. Blood streams from his nose. He looks down at Jeffrey.

Jeffrey tries to yell past him, "Janice! Janice!"

Harold turns back to yell at Janice, who is now seated on the edge of the bed, dumbstruck. "It's the same guy who was playing with your tits, Janice!"

"I know, I know."

Harold is in a fury. "I'm gonna kill him!" Harold now screams down at Jeffrey. "I'm gonna kill you!"

Jeffrey responds, "I recognize you! You're the scum-sucking swine that's been sleeping with my woman!"

Harold darts back inside. "What is with this friggin' idiot?!"

Janice gets up from the bed, sighs, walks out onto the balcony, and looks down at Jeffrey. Harold follows her.

Jeffrey sees her. "Janice, I love you! I need you! I've come to take you home to make children!"

Janice sighs.

Harold demands to know what is going on. "What the fuck is this guy's problem?!"

Janice exhales. "Apparently, he loves me, he needs me, and he wants us to make children together."

Harold senses the possibility that Janice might be somehow attracted to this maniac. "Janice! C'mon! I love you! I need you! And together, we'll make millions!"

Janice takes a moment for herself, then walks back inside. Again, Harold follows.

Janice puts on her robe, steps into her slippers, picks up her cat and her carry-all, and heads for the door.

"Janice! Where are you going?! What are you doing?!"

Janice opens the door and answers as she walks out. "I'm leaving you, Harold."

Harold follows Janice into the hallway while trying to attend to his broken nose with a handful of Kleenex. "You're leaving me for that moron?!"

"I'm sorry, Harold."

"Janice! Why?!"

Janice stops and turns around to face Harold. "Things finally came into focus: another new dress for the dance . . . or another chance to twist a guy's nose."

"What the hell are you talking about?!"

"Wish me luck, Harold. I think I'm gonna need it."

Before she turns and heads off, Janice makes a tender gesture toward Harold's nose. "I hope your nose heals up straight."

Still following after her, Harold stops at the top of the stairs leading down to the lobby. "Don't worry about me, Janice. I never liked you that much anyway!

"Hey Janice, listen to this . . . I porked your secretary!

"How do you like that, Janice! You didn't know that, did you!?

"At the Christmas party! When you were at that stupid piano singing about the little town in Bethlehem . . . I was in the accounting office porking your secretary!

"And she was great, Janice! Of course, compared to you, anybody would be great!"

As Janice passes through the lobby entrance, Harold runs back down the hallway and heads to the balcony to continue his ruckus with Jeffrey.

Janice emerges from the building and angles off for her car.

A stone's throw away, separated by the distance between the balcony and the ground, Harold and Jeffrey are at it again.

Harold screams at the top of his lungs, "If I ever get my hands on you, I'll wring your fuckin neck!"

Despite being in the freezing cold without a coat, and shivering violently, Jeffery unleashes every ounce of the clever dialogue he has previously heard delivered by his favorite cowboy heroes! "You better get your name tattooed on your ass . . . just so the undertaker knows what to write on your tombstone."

Harold has a few brilliant remarks of his own. "I'm gonna kick your ass until I get bored watching you bleed!"

Never to be outdone in the insult game, Jeffrey lays a beauty on the guy who has been sleeping with his woman, "I'll kick your ass from here to Texas. And then I'll turn you around and kick it back to wherever you think you'd like to be buried!"

Harold is up to the challenge, "Your health insurance better cover 'total ass kickings' . . . because your entire body is gonna need medical attention before I'm through!"

Jeffrey scoffs at Harold's pitiful attempt to match wits with a genius. "I could wear out a pair of boots on the ass-kicking I'm gonna give you!"

Jeffrey suddenly catches a glimpse of Janice, and immediately nothing else matters. Without hesitation, he walks away from his feud with Harold.

Janice pulls the sports car up alongside Jeffrey and opens the passenger-side door. He gets inside.

As the car heads off, Harold wins the battle of who has the last word. "That's right, run, you pathetic losers!"

Still excitable, but with no enemy to hear his rage, Harold is caught up in a momentary silent void. And realizing for the first time that there has been an audience during all this commotion, he spews his last bit of venom at the curious faces still peeking out from between curtains. "Go to bed, you . . . piss-heads!"

The faces quickly disappear, and Harold stomps into the bedroom, yanking the balcony door closed behind him.

CHAPTER TWENTY-THREE

The little red sports car turns off the highway and heads down the road towards Jeffrey's cabin. Janice is seen driving, but Jeffrey is nowhere in sight.

However, Jeffrey's voice is heard coming from inside the car, "That guy, Harold, is a very lucky man."

From a higher angle, Jeffrey is seen bent over low in his seat, with his nose dripping and his teeth chattering, as he maximizes an effort to get his hands, feet, and face, all as close to the heater as possible. "He is very, very fortunate that I didn't get my hands on him."

Janice has a rather important concern: "Jeffrey, what do you do for a living?"

"What do you mean?"

"I mean, how do you make the money that you live on?"

"I cut firewood and sell it. I've already made enough money to support my writing through this entire winter."

"And what do you do when you're not cutting firewood or writing?"

"You know, just dink around."

"I think you ought to check around for a full-time job and leave the dinking around for weekends."

"Why's that?"

"Babies cost money."

Jeffrey takes a moment to absorb the lovely inference of Janice's comment as they roll up to his front porch and park. He smiles, extracts himself from the little car, walks around it, and opens Janice's door. "C'mon, I'll show you where I caught my first fish."

"Now?"

"It's just on the other side of those boulders."

Janice doesn't really want to see where he caught a fish. "I can't–I'm not wearing snow boots." She then lifts a foot to show him her slippers.

He assures her, "It's okay, I'll carry you. Piggyback."

Jeffrey takes her hands and turns his back to her as she politely protests, "Couldn't we wait until August? When it's a little less . . . freezing?"

Jeffrey bends forward and pulls her up onto his back. "It was the first fish I ever caught in my entire life. Imagine. Last summer. Fourth of July. Hotter'n heck. I'm barefoot. Suddenly my pole quivers. I yank. And I got him!

"My first fish, from my own personal fishing hole, on my

own property! What a day that was! Sun shining, birds singing! What a day!"

And off they go, through knee-high snow, with Janice in her robe and slippers, riding piggyback. "Don't drop me."

"Nooo prob."

Holding Janice's legs up high so that her freezing feet are in no danger of touching the icy snow, Jeffrey trudges onwards, happy to tell her a little more about his fish. "My first fish, and I swear, it was at least–" Jeffrey raises his hands to show Janice how big the fish was. "At a minimum, a four-footer."

Regrettably, by raising his hands, Jeffrey releases his grip on Janice's legs, causing her feet to slide slowly down his hips and sink into the snow. "Yeowww!"

Jeffrey is mortified by his blunder and turns around to help her up out of the snow.

She instantly re-wraps her arms around his neck and jumps her legs back up over his hips, locking her feet behind his back. Jeffrey lurches backwards, forwards, and sideways, trying to maintain his footing and keep them both from toppling over. At this point, looking off over his shoulder, Janice suddenly sees what is behind the boulders: a small mountain lake of breathtaking beauty, frozen over with ice, illuminating the darkness with its brilliant moonlit sheen. "Omigod!"

Jeffrey is still humiliated by his screw-up. He cradles Janice up into his arms and tucks her feet inside his shirt. "I'm so sorry! Are your feet okay?! Are your toes okay?!"

Janice has been temporarily distracted by what she has seen. "This is your fishing hole?! You own this?!"

Jeffrey is happy to change the subject. "Yeah. It came with the cabin."

Janice's concerns have been pleasantly invigorated. "You're rich?"

Jeffrey smiles. "I've made so much money in my life you wouldn't even believe it." Janice is thrilled by this news. "Really?"

"Yep. Then I decided to buy a cabin, live in the mountains, and do something really spectacular with all the rest of my money."

"What did you do?"

"I gave it away." As this revelation settles into Janice's reality, Jeffrey proudly continues, "So now, financially speaking, I'm poor as a church mouse."

Janice squeezes out a soft whimper, "Excellent." Then, she follows up with a natural question, "And before you became really poor, how did you make the money that made you really rich?"

"I was an inventor. I invented all kinds of things. I invented a way to start a truck from inside a cabin. I invented a way to give a high-five when there's nobody else around.

"It's easy. You just figure out what people need, and then you invent it.

"Like one day, I noticed that my grandpa was always walking

around with his fly open, so I asked him why, and he said he was airing out his shorts because they were always damp.

"So I invented snap-on diapers for old people. Called 'em 'Grampers.' Old guys love 'em."

And now comes a very long pause to allow for this shocking disclosure to sink in. After which, Janice asks the most natural of follow-up questions, "Jeffrey . . . does the name Ricky Roy mean anything to you?"

"Yeah. What a jerk. Where do you know him from?"

Janice studies Jeffrey's eyes without answering.

He melts into her gaze and starts to say something, but she quickly hushes him by pressing a finger across his lips.

CHAPTER TWENTY-FOUR

The next day at Sky Tavern, Harold approaches the front desk. A large bandage covers his nose. He is not in a good mood and just wants to pay his bill and leave. "My bill."

The manager smiles. "It's already been taken care of, sir."

"Already taken care of? How's that?"

The manager pulls a set of figures up on his computer screen. "I totaled up your room charge, penthouse rate for New Year's Eve, dining expenses, added in your daughters' purchases, and they put it all on one card."

"What the hell are you talking about?" Harold looks at the screen and almost falls over. "Eighteen thousand dollars!? On my VISA card?! You must be joking!"

"Your daughters have very expensive taste in ski wear. It's all itemized on your bill."

Harold panics and reaches for his wallet, but it's gone. "Those aren't my daughters!"

The manager shrugs. "You called them your daughters. They called you their daddy. End of story as far as I'm concerned."

CURRENT AND UPCOMING BOOKS FROM THE "*12 STORIES FROM THE CAMPFIRES OF MY MIND*" SERIES BY DAVID CREPS

1
KING BOSS

Even if you are naturally inclined to shrug off life's constant parade of disappointments by simply denying their ultimate relevance, what's your method for disregarding a doctor's assurance that you will be dead within a month? For Johnny James, the King Boss, it meant he had one last chance to live. Finally.

(Now available on *Amazon*)

2
SWANKY SHAMPANE

This comedy set in Reno, Beverly Hills, and Malibu is the story of Best Actress nominee, Swanky Shampane, a two-timing, double-dealing, poetically-profane, ridiculously-neurotic, but fabulously charming, former cat house prostitute, obsessed with changing her public image prior to the night of the Academy Awards when she will be taking the front-row-center-seat next to her bitterest rival, "that filthy bitch" . . . Myrtle Street.

3
THE NEW YEAR'S RESOLUTION

A romantic comedy concerning the last two people a merciful God would ever put together under one roof, especially during the week that one of them is giving up cigarettes. It's what happens when ridiculously neurotic egos do battle while under the pressures of a calm biological attraction.

(Now available on *Amazon*)

4
THE OTHER BROTHERS

A Disney-style comedy about two twelve-year-old boys. One black. One white. One from the mean streets of Harlem, one from an isolated chicken farm in Nevada.

Both too young to be full-fledged con artists, but both already in abundant possession of the devilish charm and swagger necessary for the calling should their lives continue along their current paths.

And were it not for their love of basketball and their mutual respect for the way each other plays the game, these two big-talkers might never have made it to the brotherhood that bonds them into a lifetime of friendship.

5
MARGARITAVILLE

Is the story of two bungling con artists living on a pathetic excuse for a sailboat, in a trailer park, while looking for that one big score that will get them to the warm, turquoise waters and sandy, white beaches of the Caribbean, where they can live "just like Jimmy Buffet."

6
THE ROAD TO JACK'S HOUSE

The story of a thirty-six-year-old virgin who has a very assertive opinion on every matter under the sun. And the guy who, at the time of meeting this woman, is engaged in a search for the answer to the question, "What is the best way for me to live the rest of my life?"

They are both a little pissy, both a little self-righteous, and they each have their own personal agendas when they head down Highway 395 to take her screenplay to Hollywood, where she has good reason to believe that it will be read by Jack Nicholson. At his house. On a Saturday afternoon–while she is swimming in his pool, during a star-studded, rollicking-romp of a barbeque.

7
LAST CHANCE

A chilling comedy about the possibilities of "what if?" What if the focus of present-day science were trained on finding a way to eliminate all violent tendencies from human behavior?

And what if a relatively small group of well-funded scientists undertook this problem, in secret, and through genetic engineering were successful in solving it?

And what if they not only discovered the formula for making humanity a passive species, but at the same time realized a way to dispense this formula throughout the world–without notice and without permission? Should they?

(Now available on *Amazon*)

8
THE GREATEST MOVIE EVER WRITTEN

The attempt by an artist of questionable sanity to write and direct a movie that will literally "save the world." The pressure is great. The time is short. And by every initial indication, his thinking is way too far "outside the box."

Yet he perseveres, fueled by a single belief: "You can't prevent the human race from destroying itself with a bigger, better weapon. But if your thoughts are crazy enough . . . you might be able to do it with an idea."

9
THE REUNION

The story of what happens when a thirty-year class reunion brings together five old high school friends who have been suffering from the same secret guilt from so many years ago.

It is also the story of what happens when Elizabeth Maryann Walker spends her weekend with these same five guys, up in the mountains, camping at Bennies Creek, falling in love for the second time in her life–with the same man.

10
THE IRONY OF IT ALL

A story of what might have happened during the last few weeks of the 2000 presidential election if the writer, Chesterfield Johnson, a man of unusual perceptions and bizarre solutions, had convinced candidate Al Gore to act in accordance with Chesterfield's unsolicited advice.

Besides his strategy to win Mr. Gore the election, Chesterfield has also devised a strategy to get his latest screenplay into the hands of an aging actress desperate to find a script worthy of her talent.

And within these dual tracks of Chesterfield's efforts, live an assortment of schemers and manipulators operating in the guise of Hollywood agents, political insiders, tabloid celebrities, and talk show hosts.

THE NEW YEAR'S RESOLUTION

11
ON THE WALL IN THE CAVE

This comedy explores the absurdities of what can happen when a seemingly normal American man goes into a cave in the mountains to meditate on the problems of the world with the intention of figuring out the solution to the whole mess.

Current news headlines from any part of the world make this character's mindset very easy to understand.

12
THE SWEET REDEMPTION OF REPREHENSIBLE BOB

This is the story of a reprehensible human being with an insatiable need to fondle breasts at every possibility. With or without permission.

And the lovely woman who had suffered enormously for twenty years, before deciding to track him down and "shoot him through the eyeballs."

(Now available on *Amazon*)

ABOUT DAVID CREPS

David Creps has worked as a ditch-digger, truck driver, dice-dealer, carpenter, screenwriter, playwright, and novelist.

The first highlight of his writing career happened when he was twenty-two years old, and Shecky Greene read a couple pages of his stuff, and said, "I've read worse."

And, in analyzing the unspoken words within Shecky's comment, David understood Shecky to mean, "Holy crap! I am the greatest writer Shecky has ever allowed to work for him for free!"

This was enough to inspire him through decades of laborious scribbling and ultimately provide him with enough cash to get a small mortgage on a cabin 8,000 feet up in the mountains, and to purchase a genuine 1966 greenish-gray (a color occasionally referred to, behind his back, as puke-green) U.S. Postal Service mail truck lined with wall-to-wall-to-ceiling-to-floor green shag carpet, which could transport more lengths of lumber in one haul than any vehicle in this entire country.

David is also a husband, a father, a brother, a grandfather, and a good-natured (and occasionally totally innocent) rascal.

Made in the USA
Middletown, DE
15 May 2021